The audiobook for THE NAME HENNESSY is now available where all major audiobooks are sold.

THE NAME HENNESSY

Benjamin Boucvalt

Ghost Light Publishing

WINONA

THE NAME HENNESSY

Published by Ghost Light Publishing

First edition: June 11, 2024 ISBN: 978-0-9903334-3-2

Edited by Jill Krase
Instagram: @ovenbirdbindery

Cover illustrations and design by Jonathan Marks Barravecchia
JonathanMarksArt.com   Instagram: @jonathanmarksart

Interior illustrations by Helena Scholz-Carlson
Instagram: @helenasc.art

First Nation and Native language resource:
Native Languages of the Americas   Native-Languages.org
Shoshoni Language Project

For my brothers,
Christopher, Matthew, and Andrew

And Jonathan . . . You crazy son of a bitch
It was you

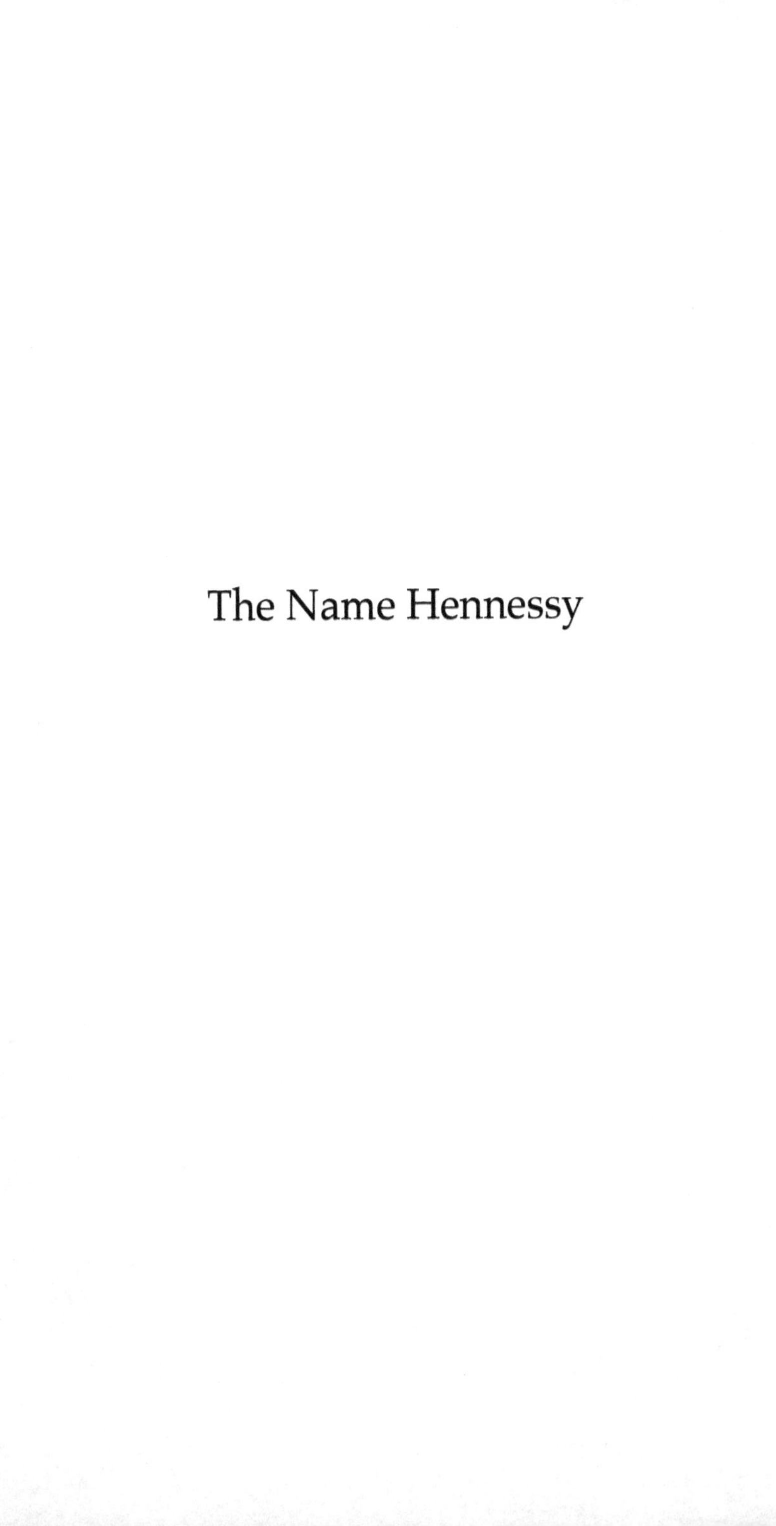

The Name Hennessy

"You go in there you'll die, woman."

I ignored the man's warning and the gunshots that accompanied it as I marched down the road toward the building with my long skirt spinning up a dusty cloud behind me. The bullets were blasting through the bitter air, and a red sun was almost gone behind the mountains. They all said this day would come. But I kept driving forward and never looked to the men gathered outside in the twilight. They barricaded themselves behind toppled wagons and wooden crates, anything that could shield them from the menace holing up inside the town's parlor. A wooden building at the center of the town, where the men gathered to drink and gamble. Blindly, they fired into the darkness beyond its windows.

Still, my eyes were fixed only on the door of the parlor, clenching the long rifle in my hands. I didn't stop, even as the bullets pierced the wooden walls around it. Everything in my being screamed for me to turn back. To rip that silver star from my blouse and throw it to the road. Those who knew of this town would have agreed with the men. And I would have too, if not for the firestorm and the whisper that consumed my mind. It was that voice that pushed me on, until I was standing with my back to the door.

One man yelled from across the road with a shake in his voice, "Ya go through that door, you're on your own."

The men lit torches to prepare for the coming night, and a fiery glow washed over the road. I pulled the rifle into my chest as I steadied my breath. Looking out to the homes and storefronts about me, I saw a place that used to be filled with my welcoming neighbors and inviting friends. But now, it was littered with the beady eyes of them crouched in hiding. Creeping around corners and spying from the rooftops. Some men stayed inside with all the women other than me, hanging at the edges of the window frames and peering from behind the curtains.

I didn't hate them for it. It's just who they were now. Believing in too many stories, tall tales of a man who couldn't be killed. *But those stories are not true*, I thought.

I put my hand on the badge on my chest, trying to slow down my racing heart. The trees in the valley were rising up around me, and the town was beginning to sink, and soon the land would swallow us whole. I looked to the badge I wore, took one last deep breath, closed my eyes, and whispered, *"He's just a man."*

Then, to all those hiding and taking cover, I vanished as I pushed through the door.

I dove into the deserted parlor, deserted except for the one who had caused all the men to scatter. The place was filled with empty tables and chairs. Right away I flipped over a card table and took cover behind it. I reached over the table with the rifle and fired a few shots blindly across the room and took cover again. With each blast from my rifle, an image flashed before me. This image came to me often. A sky on fire. And a horizon in flames.

I took a few quick breaths and started to reach over the table again, but the rifle jammed. I shook the weapon and frantically yanked on its lever to no avail, banging on its side with my fist.

"Stupid thing," I cursed.

I threw the rifle to the ground and pulled out the six-shooter holstered at my hip. I clasped it with two hands, catching my reflection in its silver barrel. Or maybe I saw a flash of fire. I couldn't remember anymore. I looked up to the stairs and wooden railing above, but I couldn't spot any movement.

Where is he?

To the other side of the parlor, I saw that no one was behind the bar. Just liquor bottles and half-empty glasses. The place was thick with the smell of cigar smoke and all the remnants of a scene people had just left in a hurry. Broken shards from the shattered windows. Poker chips and playing cards from the table now lay all around me.

This was my first time in the parlor. Women were never allowed in here.

GUNSHOT.

Another blast rang out from outside the parlor. I flinched even though I had figured the men's bullets wouldn't stop coming once I entered the building. That would've been wishful thinking.

I tried to yell over the blasts. "Hennessy!" GUNSHOT. "There's nowhere ta go. I know ya in here. I'm gonna—" GUNSHOT. "I'm gonna need ya ta—" GUNSHOT. "I'm gonna need ya ta come —" GUNSHOT. "Jesus Christ." GUNSHOT. "STOP," I yelled to the men outside.

The whole place suddenly fell silent. I listened for the sound of breathing or rustling but heard nothing. I slowly peered over the top of the table to survey the room. The mirror above the fireplace now had bullet holes in it, as did the polished banister next to the stairs. Across the parlor was another table toppled over in a similar fashion to mine, but there was no way to see what was behind it.

My words didn't come out at first, but then finally, "Which one of ya am I dealin' with?"

Nothing.

"Daniel? Daniel, that you in here? Christian? Ya let me know."

Silence.

"Or are . . . are ya . . . . You Jonah? You the one they call the—"

I stopped myself. Not wanting to give power to that name. I took a breath and continued.

"We're sorry for what happened to your . . . . She was a good woman. She uhhh . . . . . What business do ya have? Honestly, ya surprised the hell out of all of us ridin' in here. Ya here ta try ta kill us? Get killed yourself? Because no one out there wants that. I don't want that. I can tell ya true. No one here is lookin' to kill anyone."

GUNSHOT.

I swore under my breath, "God damn it." After a moment I called again. "Hennessy?"

I heard a long, slow sigh but couldn't tell for sure from where it came. My ears sharpened, trying to discover where the breath was coming from. Then from the other side of the parlor came a low, scratchy voice. One that hadn't spoken for some time.

"I'm here."

I could not only hear the voice, but I could feel it. It rolled like a wave across the floor and crashed right into my body.

"Ya behind that there table?" I asked.

"I am."

"You a Hennessy, right?" I needed to be sure.

"I am."

"*Shit. Okay,*" I said softly. It got hard for me to breathe. All the tales that I had heard about the name Hennessy flooded into my mind. If I was going to make it through this, I would have to lock the stories out. Or else, I would be a slave to them like all those outside. I ordered, "I'm gonna need ya to come out."

"Yeah, I don't see how that's much of a good idea on account of being shot at and all."

"I ain't shot at ya. And I ain't gonna shoot ya."

"You ain't shot at me?"

"No."

"Ya sure? It sure did sound like someone firin' in here."

"Ain't no one in here firing. Ya just need to come out where I can see ya."

"What assurance do I have that ya ain't lyin'?"

"My word," I said.

"Your word?"

"My word. I give ya my . . ." But before I could swear, the color was leaving my face and my head started to spin.

"What's that?"

"I give ya my . . . ." I swallowed some air and put my hand to my stomach, trying to keep my insides still. Hot bile was starting to burn the back of my throat.

"You okay over there?"

"Oh, god." I heaved. *Not like this*, I thought. *Please God, not like this.* I heaved again.

"Hey, you gonna throw up?"

"No."

"Why don't ya just take a few deep breaths? Just breathe."

"Shut up. You don't be telling me what ta do."

"Alright," said the voice.

"Okay, okay," I said, taking a few deep breaths, reluctantly doing as he suggested. The spinning slowed and the heaving subsided. Regaining some balance, I swallowed my spit and yelled to him, "As the sheriff of this town, I'm orderin' ya ta come out."

"Sheriff?"

"Yes. And I'm orderin' ya ta come out."

"No offense, Sheriff, but ya sound like a woman."

"I am a woman."

"A woman sheriff?"

"Yes."

"Why do y'all have a woman sheriff?"

"Jesus Christ. Listen, ya either come out now with me, or we wait until this room is filled with armed men."

"So, you're tellin' me—a group of men—are about ta fill this room—led by their lady sheriff?"

"Yes."

"Yeah, that don't sound right."

The overwhelming sense that I was about to spew my insides onto the floor was replaced by a swelling rage. And not because he was wrong, but because he was right, that the men were unlikely to join me in the parlor. I looked up to the chandelier above me, infuriated that it was only now that I finally got a chance to see its crystals flickering in the light. Only now did they allow me to go in. When no one else wanted to. I was alone and I didn't have to be. My breath became hot. "You don't know what those men are willin' to do, Hennessy," I said.

"Oh, yeah? And what about you? You care if I make it out alive?"

"That's my job."

"That ain't what I asked."

It sure wasn't. But I pressed on. "Let's get to it now. Come out."

"Ya know there's a sayin' I hear y'all have become fond of. One that ain't sittin' well with me at the moment."

"I don't know what ya talkin' about." But I did. Everyone did. It might as well have been a sign that hung at the entrance to the town.

"The only good Hennessy is . . ."

"Let's go, we don't have time for this," I said.

"Come on, say it."

"Say what?"

"Whatcha thinkin'. What those men out there are thinkin'."

"I don't know what they're thinkin'."

"Come on now. Finish it," said the voice.

I wouldn't say what he wanted me to and instead yelled out to him, "I'm gonna give ya ta the count of five to come out."

"The only good Hennessy . . ."

"One. Two."

"Say it, lady."

"Don't ya call me 'lady'. I'm the sheriff. Three. Four."

"The only good Hennessy . . . is . . ."

"FIVE," I demanded.

" . . . Say it."

Admitting to it wasn't going to help my cause. I didn't want to provoke him. But there was no getting around it. He knew. I knew. They all knew. "The only good Hennessy is a dead Hennessy."

The voice said, "Yeah. I think I'll just stay right here."

There was no way I could stand up now, especially since I knew for sure that the person behind the other table was a Hennessy. The best thing I could do was to find out which one of them he was. It would determine the danger of the company I now kept. "Who are ya?"

"I'm a Hennessy."

"Yeah, but *which one*?" I asked. The name Hennessy didn't always bring with it such fear. There was once a time when it wasn't all like this. When the Hennessys gave you a feeling that was different. But now they had become . . . darker. Some of them more than others.

"I think ya know that, ma'am."

"Yeah? Why don't ya confirm that for me?" I looked about the parlor to see if I could take better cover. Behind the bar would've been good, but that was too far away now. I was stuck behind that table.

"Where are those men of yours, Sheriff?"

"They're comin'."

"Sure they are."

"They're comin'." I was trying to make myself believe it. I did hope. But I knew what ruled those men. I had come not to expect much from them.

"Why don't you come out instead?"

"Oh, I bet ya'd love that."

"Come on."

"I know what ya are."

"Do ya?" asked the voice.

I did. And I didn't. What was true and what had simply become story had blurred. The line between the possible and the impossible had vanished. What was a man truly capable of and what were just stories that people had come to believe? The two rode along together, side by side in a whirlwind of fear and anger that had swept up this town. We were living in a nightmare that we couldn't escape. But I told myself to believe in what I could see. And the dead tell no lies.

"I know what ya've done," I said.

"I bet ya do, ma'am."

"Never trust a Hennessy."

The voice softened. "Listen, I'm here ta help ya."

"I'm not lookin' for help."

"Come out."

"YOUR NAME," I ordered.

"Okay. I give ya my name, and you come out."

"I ain't said that. Ya name."

"Will it matter?"

"Your name."

Silence fell. I wasn't getting anywhere like this. Doubt was creeping in as I sat trapped, unable to see a way of even getting out of there. Running back out through the door would be like running into a firing squad. The men outside were so on edge, they would've fired at the slightest movement coming out that door, thinking it could be Hennessy, no matter which one. And there was no telling who or what exactly was barricaded across the room. The cool evening air filled my lungs and sent a chill through my body. *Why the hell did I come in so fast?* I thought. All the men finished running out before I came charging in. Then, as I was succumbing to the idea that I just might die behind that table, the voice said, "Daniel."

The name made my whole body go still. I confirmed, "Daniel?"

"Daniel, ma'am."

I took a cautious breath, and my head fell back as I sighed it out. A warm feeling grew from inside my chest, and it melted the chill that had overcome me. It had been so long, and they all looked so alike. But this being Daniel, I thought, *Thank God.* As I was beginning to feel some of the tension leave me, it rushed back with a sudden squeeze when I thought again, *Never trust a Hennessy.*

"Now come on out, ma'am," said the voice.

"I ain't comin' out."

"Listen, I told ya my name, now ya come out."

"I never agreed to that. Why would I do that?"

"Someone has to come out."

"Ya think that makes sense? Ya gave me your name and now ya think I'm gonna come out?"

"I gave ya somethin'."

"It's not like ya threw your gun away or anythin'. Ya gave me a name."

"I ain't movin'."

"Well, shit. You're somethin' crazy if ya think those two things are equal. They're not equal. A name for a name is equal. Not me walkin' out there so ya can shoot me. Ya want fair? Charolette. That's my name. There. Now we're back ta where we started."

The voice paused before eventually saying, "Charolette?"

"Yes."

"Charolette Crowley?"

"*Sheriff* Charolette Crowley." I immediately regretted saying this. It didn't matter who I was. I was the sheriff. My name wasn't any of his concern. No matter who he was.

"Sheriff Charolette Crowley. My god. Of course ya are," said the voice. "You know me."

"All I know is that you're a Hennessy."

"No. You know me. It's been a while, but we have history."

"No we don't."

"We do," insisted the voice.

I was lying. I did have a memory of Daniel from long ago. It was a brief moment in time. We all knew of each other when we were younger than we were now. A lot younger. But it was Daniel that

I remembered the most. He and all his brothers had a reputation in the town back in those days, especially among the women who fancied them. I could recall how the ladies would blush and put their hands on the Hennessy boys' broad shoulders, laughing at everything they said. That wasn't me. But my memory of Daniel was fond. Though, that memory wasn't enough to put me at ease or to toss aside my reasons for being there.

"I don't want nothin' to do with any Hennessys," I said.

"Charolette. Ya must remember me."

"I don't."

"You don't?"

"I don't."

"Right. Of course, you don't. Ya foolin' yourself, ma'am."

"*Sheriff.* I am the sheriff. One who knows better than ta ever trust a Hennessy."

"I ain't gonna hurt anyone. I am who I say I am."

"Yeah? How do I know ya ain't lyin'?"

"You know I ain't lyin'."

"How do I know ya ain't *him*?"

"Because if I were him, you'd be dead. You'd be lyin' on the floor with a hole through your heart."

All the air in the room was gone. A wave of terror washed away everything else, and only this image of my demise remained. My body lying next to the green felted table I had been hiding behind, my back sinking into the broken glass, the glow from the torches spilling through the window reflecting in my dead eyes, the chandelier swaying gently above me, and the hole in my heart filling the floor beneath me with blood.

It was true. I'd be dead if this weren't Daniel. Had it been Jonah, I wouldn't have made it this far. My actions would've needed to be faster than they had been. I opened my mouth to speak, but nothing came out while I was paralyzed by these thoughts.

The voice from across the room rumbled on. The scratchiness was now gone. It became firm and steady. It grabbed me, pulling me in as if his words were my own. Like a sermon quoting a gospel or a verse that was all too familiar. "Let me see. Three men shot outside a saloon in Prescott, a rancher found beaten and stripped of his clothes, one man found eaten alive by coyotes after being tied to a red rock in New Mexico, one man with a bullet in his head at an outpost near Kansas City. And the list goes on. And as I rode in this mornin', I hear ya can add to that list two Pinkerton detectives and one U.S. marshal. That sound about right?"

He wasn't lying. Jonah's list of victims kept growing and growing. And with each new addition, so did the stories you'd hear.

"*Right,*" I said hesitantly. I looked over the table again. All was still save for the flickering candles on the wall.

The Hennessy boys had left this town many years ago. They went on a hunt for the man who had killed Jonah's wife. And as Jonah's brother, Daniel went along. Vowing never to come back until they found what they were looking for. Some reckless souls dared to go out after them from time to time, thinking the reward was worth their lives. But not me. I've been waiting. Knowing that one day, even the worst of us will manage to find our way back home.

"If you're Daniel, then where is Jonah?"

"Still haven't seen him, have ya? Heartbreakin'. I bet ya want to get ya hands on him real bad. A man like that. Tired of waitin', I bet. Hell, I know I'm tired. All those dark nights in the valleys, in the desert. I think about them searchers, staring up at that big old night sky, saying to themselves, 'That son of a bitch could be anywhere.' I know ya hesitant to speak to me, but seein' as ya don't have much to go on, ya might want to listen. No one's ever gonna catch him. No one's ever gonna find him. Not until he's ready to be found. He's gone too deep. Lost. His eyes have changed. His heart is . . . it's . . . . I can help ya. I ain't hidin' him. But I can give ya what ya want. I can bring ya peace."

"No deals, Hennessy."

"I have everything ya need to know. Everything. And you'll never worry about him again."

"Daniel, ya know I can't—"

"—He's comin', Charolette." The sharp voice cut me off. It spoke as a harbinger. As if it were an omen. Words that I had heard far too often. A warning I refused to fear. "Jonah is comin'. You need to let me help you."

"He's comin'?"

"Napusai Pitsih."

He spoke words in a native tongue. From a tribe north of here. It was a language that I did not speak, but I knew well what these words meant. We all knew.

"The Nightmare," I whispered to myself. It was the name that I had tried not to speak but that somehow always managed to find its way to my tongue. Even saying it now, I found the room seemed darker. Night was now upon us. It was as they all had feared. "He's coming."

"And fire will follow. I'm givin' you a chance, Charolette. To put an end ta all this. I know you don't wanna do it, but you need ta trust me."

I had gotten used to not trusting. People never really gave me good reason to. But I didn't have much of a choice if Daniel was the only one with information. All I had was him. And if Jonah was coming, it would awaken the darkest part of me, the part of me that might sacrifice the rule of law despite this badge.

I could feel myself already being pulled into their world. A world where the rules of men were bent. A place where not all was what it seemed to be. It was a place I refused to let myself go, because in that world, I stood no chance.

"God damn it," I said to myself. "Shit. You can do this." I didn't allow myself to contend with the idea of what Jonah had become. The Nightmare, as they called him. But Daniel was right. I was afraid. There was a flash, and my vision filled with flames. I looked up and the roof to the parlor was gone, and I saw out into the night sky and a line of fire screeched across it like a comet. Then the whisper that had driven me this far came to me again. A voice rolling about in the infinite space of my mind. As if the voice itself could reach out and grab my head and focus my eyes, demanding I see what it wanted me to see. And to that persistent voice I promised, "Yes. You will." I turned my head and spoke up over my shoulder, "Okay, Daniel. I'm trustin' ya. Just don't . . . kill me, okay?"

"Alright."

"Not all that comfortin', but thank you." I holstered my gun and slowly stood up.

No one appeared from the other side of the parlor. Immediately I felt an impulse to dive back behind the table, but I fought and stood firm. I briefly clenched the star on my chest and lifted my head.

"I'm out," I said.

"And ya gun?"

"I ain't holdin' it."

"Fair enough."

His last words rumbled and faded about the place until it was silent. Then from across the room I heard movement, and a chair slid on the wood floor from behind the other table. A dark figure rose up. It stood right before me, but all I could see was the shadow of a man. A ghost in the darkness. It seemed to hover there, and an iciness rolled up my spine. I had seen this image before. It came to me in the dead of night when I lay awake, floating above my frozen body. The powerlessness I felt during those many nights returned to me now. Like I no longer had command of my body and something beyond me controlled my fate.

Then the shadow moved. It glided towards me, sucking the air from my body as it grew closer. And just when I was starting to feel its grip take over my heart, I could breathe again when I saw Hennessy step out into the light, becoming illuminated.

The shadow faded away, and what I now saw was just a man. His clothes were those of one who had made the road his home for some time. His tall stature was familiar to me, but it was not until he raised the brim of his hat that I knew, when I could see the light in his eyes, that it was Daniel. Eyes like a green ember, haloed in blue. Though my memories of him were few, this was one of them. My heartbeat was steady. But I did not lose sight of where I was or who I was with and the danger I was still in.

"So, what do ya have to tell me?" I asked. But he didn't give me information. Turns out he had some questions of his own.

"How's my family?"

"I don't know."

"Have you seen my other brothers?"

"No."

"My father? Have ya heard anything about my father?"

"I stay away from the Hennessys."

"It's important for me to know he's alright."

"As far as I know."

"As far as you know, huh?" Hennessy nodded. It was going to have to be enough for him. I could see he was worried about his family that was still here. The rest of his brothers and parents had been keeping quiet these days. And I really hadn't heard much.

Hennessy looked down towards his waist when he saw my eyes were glued to the gun hanging from his hip. I was focusing so hard that a dizziness, like standing on the edge of a cliff, overwhelmed me. I'm sure he could tell I was still nervous. It's not what I observed in him, though. His movements were glacial, if he moved at all. He took a breath, and with measured caution spoke carefully and slowly, "I'm gonna reach inside my pocket."

"No," I ordered.

"I need ta go inside my pocket."

"Don't do it, Hennessy."

"Daniel," he offered.

"What does it matter what I call ya? You and ya brothers are all the same."

"Ya know that's not true."

"I don't."

The name Hennessy had taken on a life of its own ever since the two of those boys had left. And though Daniel wasn't Jonah, he rode with Jonah. He was Jonah's brother. It was hard separating one from the other. Though, at that moment, I did think of how the Nightmare would scalp men alive and watch them bake in the hot sun. The thought made the top of my head start to burn.

Hennessy broke the silence. "What? We're just gonna stare at each other all day?"

Yes, I thought, we would. Because there was no way I was about to let him reach under his coat. To watch his hand move slowly toward where his weapon sat. Our staring continued until another idea finally came to him.

"Okay, I'm gonna take my gun off and put it on the table."

I nodded. Hennessy did, too. Then, like pushing through molasses, Hennessy's hand slowly moved to the buckle on his belt. I watched every subtle shift of his fingers as he unfastened it. Hennessy lifted his gun belt up and put it on top of the table standing in between us. He gently lifted his hat from his head and placed it down as well. The shadows were gone from his face as he backed away from the table.

"How about now?"

"Go ahead," I allowed. But as Hennessy began to reach inside his jacket, I yelled, "Wait! What if that's not your only one?"

"Why don't ya just point ya gun at me, Charolette?"

"Sheriff. I'm the goddamn sheriff. Okay?" I never should have told him my name. But hearing it on his tongue was reminding me. Reminding me of why we were all there. I pulled out my gun and aimed it at him.

"Better?" he asked.

"Slowly."

I wanted Hennessy to believe that I'd pull the trigger. That I was ready. That there was a need living behind my eyes, like I was hoping for him to give me a reason. But he wouldn't give me one. His hand floated to the inside of his jacket and pulled out a thick envelope. Hennessy held it out in his hands. It was too big for a simple letter, and whatever was inside had some weight.

"What the hell is that?"

"Everything ya need to know is inside this envelope."

"Give it ta me."

"I need ya ta listen ta me first."

"If you know about that monster, ya need to tell me what's goin' on."

"Monster?"

"If he's comin' here—"

"Ya mean my brother?"

"Your brother is a monster. If ya have anything that can help us. Ya need ta tell me."

"I will. After ya listen. What's inside will mean nothin' if ya don't."

"Do ya know why I'm in here alone? Because every god damn man in this town is terrified. Thinkin' your brother, this man called the Nightmare, has his eye on this place. Believing that death is comin' for them. And they think ya brother's in here now. They think you're him. You were right. No one is comin' in here ta help me. But ya know what they're gonna do? If I don't come out soon with ya, they're gonna burn this place down with you in it. Me too, if they have ta. So we don't have time for all this."

Hennessy held his hands up and took a cautious step toward me. "Somethin's happened. And ya need ta know the truth. The Hennessys deserve ta have the truth told. Charolette, please."

But he's comin', I thought. And though I was suppressing an urge to snatch the envelope from his hands, I knew it wouldn't matter. I needed to hear him. The weariness in his eyes told me of a darkness that he was holding back. I recognized it. What was in those eyes and what was in that envelope intrigued me greatly.

"Okay . . . Daniel. I'm listenin'."

"Do you believe in destiny, Charolette?"

"I don't know."

"Do ya think fate has brought ya here? Why is it you're in here and no one else?"

"Because everyone else is afraid."

"And you're not?"

"I don't believe in ghosts."

"But you see 'em, surely."

I tried not to think of Jonah as anything otherworldly. He was nothing more than a shadow, but a shadow that plagued my dreams. "He's no ghost," I said under my breath.

"What's that?" Daniel wondered aloud about what I had said as he caught the murmur I made.

I was haunted by someone who no longer walked among us. A dishonored soul that would come to me in fire and speak in my mind. Always with the same message. But that was not for Hennessy to know. "Let's get to it," I said.

Hennessy looked through the broken glass of the front window and, from a distance, tried to see out into the road. He seemed to see something out beyond the flicker of torches and the fading of dusk. Something that only he could see.

"It happened right across the way," he said. "Where he watched her die. We were all drinkin' together. I was with Jonah and his lady. That's when it all began. When that murderer got away."

"Did y'all find 'im?"

"He's still out there."

"Is your brother still lookin' for 'im?"

Hennessy turned back from looking out the window, like coming back to the present with me, with my gun still aimed at his chest.

"I'm sorry, Charolette. I'm sorry for what happened to ya."

"I would appreciate it if ya called me Sheriff."

"Why are ya wearin' his badge? Is that his iron, too?"

Hennessy eyed the star pinned to my chest. He had seen it before but not on me. And as he stared at it, I felt as if it stared right back at him. It had been waiting with me for the Hennessys this whole time. It never stopped. Here they met again, this badge and this Hennessy, back where they last found themselves together.

I broke his gaze. "Daniel. I'm listenin'. Did your brother find 'im?"

"The thing I think ya have ta understand about my brother is that he loved this town. And the people in it. And god, he loved his wife. When she was murdered out that way, I think a part of him died with her."

"We've all lost someone."

"I know, Charolette. I know. That's what I'm trying ta say. I'm sorry."

"Don't you dare apologize. Not for him."

"No, of course not. When ya husband died, that wasn't easy for any of us. Crowley was—"

"Careful, Hennessy," I threatened. This was it. The thing that drove me on and pushed me through that door and into the fire. But I didn't want to talk about my husband. Not with anyone, and especially not him. No one had earned the right.

"Your husband's death was an accident," Hennessy said.

"A bullet in the chest is not an accident."

"Crowley put that iron in front of Jonah."

"My husband was trying to stop him."

"Stop him from what? From going after a murderer?"

"No. From becoming one."

"That bastard ended his wife's life. Trying to put an end to *him* wouldn't have made Jonah a killer."

"Yes, it would've."

When my husband was sheriff, he went after the Hennessys before they got too far. He wanted to keep them from taking matters into their own hands. But Jonah wouldn't let anything get in his way. I continued, "Crowley would've helped him. All Jonah had to do was stop."

"His wife was taken from him. Passion, rage, name it what ya want, but he was called upon. It would've called on any of us. Crowley got in the way of justice."

"Yeah? What about the others?"

Hennessy hesitated for a second. ". . . That was different."

"Different how?"

He looked as though his vision was blurring and his eyes were being filled with the blood of the men they had killed, dizzying him, as if everything in the room was becoming red. I wondered about what his answer would be, and how it would've been different if his brother was answering.

He reached out to put his hand on one of the tables to balance himself. Then rubbed his forehead and ran his fingers through his hair as he said, "We're moving too fast. Let me . . . . Let's just calm down for a second."

"I'm calm."

"Why don't you put his gun away?"

"Because I'm not an idiot."

"Charolette. I know it's easier ta pretend that ya don't know me."

"I don't."

"Ya know I'm not gonna hurt ya. And if I wanted ta kill ya I would've done it already. Let's just take the tension off this a bit."

No one would have put their gun down, not with a Hennessy. And though he had yet to reveal anything worthwhile, I would do it. Not because it was wise. But because Hennessy did it first. Surely I could stand in a room with an unarmed man.

No one imagined I could take this on. No one saw me for who I really was. Not *one* soul in this town had believed in me. *I can do this*, I thought. Then I holstered the gun I had been holding and began to unbuckle my belt. I stared at him as I started to walk toward the table where his gun lay. *I'm not afraid.* I placed the weapon on top of his. Moving away from it was harder than putting it down, but I steeled myself and backed off. We stood apart from each other, just one man and one woman, with the power of lead and gunpowder now sitting in between us. Breaking the standoff, I began to move about the parlor, trying my best to trust him as he trusted me.

"If I wanted ta kill you, I would've done it already, too. And I don't know you."

"I know," he conceded.

"Keep talkin'."

Hennessy, too, was now moving, walking opposite of me. He stepped around the furniture and picked up one of the fallen chairs and stood it upright. He caught his reflection in the mirror. A bullet hole that had gone through it covered half of his face. I don't think he had seen his reflection for some time. I watched him as he rubbed his hand over his eyes and gazed into the mirror again, as if he thought he'd see something new. He suddenly felt me staring at him, and he turned from the mirror and continued about the place.

"You're right. My brother has changed."

"I wouldn't get so close to that window," I warned.

Hennessy stopped just before he came into view of the men outside. Right into the sights of all those cowering behind their wagons, with their shaky barrels aimed, waiting for something to move. His gaze tracked from the broken window to the shattered glass on the floor, and he backed away.

"But Jonah's not the only one who's changed. This town. And everyone in it. It's changed. And me. Even you, Charolette."

"Everything changes."

"Look out there. I don't even recognize it anymore. I remember running' through these streets as a kid."

"Y'all were mischief."

Hennessy seemed excited by my slight acknowledgement of the past. "That's right. Maybe we stole one too many times from the candy jars. But it never looked like this. It's dark and dead out there. It seems the sun barely shines on it anymore. Y'all must miss it, right? I can't be the only one."

I tried to keep him on the topic at hand. "What does any of this have to do with Jonah?"

"Everything."

"You stallin'?"

"I ain't stallin'. I just think it's important ta know we all have some answering ta do."

"Maybe. But not ta you."

I could tell he was trying to reach me, to find some common ground. But I was only concerned with one thing since my husband died, and the only voice I had been listening to was his. Despite all this, even though I tried to lock away the memory I had of Daniel, I felt he could see it. That he saw my resistance.

"Charolette. Can ya try ta remember? How old were we?"

"Too young to remember."

"We were young. I gave ya some licorice once. Not far from here. Down near Chelsea's Creek. I think you were like fourteen or somethin'."

"Fifteen."

"Yeah. I thought you were real pretty."

I hadn't been called pretty in a long time. I hadn't thought of myself in that way in recent years, nor did I care all that much about things like that anymore. But hearing it now, hearing what he thought of me back then, before all of this, it awakened a part of me. And I felt a fondness for that moment in time grow inside me. I would like to have known that then, when we stood together by the water. But that was a long time ago, and that was no longer this world.

"I don't know what you're talkin' about, Daniel. And I'm not here to relive memories. Jonah. Tell me about J—"

GUNSHOT. GUNSHOT. GUNSHOT. The wall spat chips of wood in my face as another onslaught of bullets came ripping through. We took cover like we were hiding from lightning in a thunderstorm. Each piece of lead leaving whispers for us as they cut across the air.

"Son of a bitch," I cried. "I'm in here, you assholes!"

I felt a sudden hot bite in my forearm. I didn't look, telling myself the hurt couldn't be much and covering the spot that burned with my hand. I held my hand there, breathing a few deep breaths, until the parlor went silent as the gunfire from outside stopped again.

Hennessy looked over to me, "You alright?"
"Damn it."
"Let me look at it."
"I'm fine."

Hennessy crawled across the floor to me, careful to clear under the window so as to not be seen, being more careful now than he had been before, pushing aside pieces of glass and debris.

"Is it your arm?" He asked as he reached out for it.

"Hey! Get your goddamn hands away from me."

"Alright, alright. It go through?"

"It's nothing."

"That's blood."

I looked down. Blood was beginning to seep between my fingers and drip to the ground as I held pressure.

"Yeah. So?"

"You don't have to be proud."

"To hell with you, it's a nick."

"I can wrap it."

"It don't need wrappin'. It's a nick."

"Then why you still holdin' it?" He waited for an answer, but received none. "Come on."

He was earnest. And he wasn't going to shut up about it. *Could I let him do this?* I eyed Hennessy. *No tricks*, I thought. He's just going to wrap it.

"You be careful, Daniel," I warned. "Real careful."

Hennessy went to the bar and grabbed a bottle of whiskey and a towel, ripping it in half. He crawled back toward me with the towel in his mouth.

"So, you've undoubtedly done this before," I stated.

"It's come up."

He put his hand around my wrist, but I wouldn't let him pull my hand away from the wound. Until his eyes looked up at me. They told me I'd be safe. So I let him. As he removed my hand, blood rolled down the sides of my forearm. It was hard to see anything else. All that red. Hennessy took the bottle of whiskey and washed the blood off my forearm and out of the wound. A tight exhale came out through my nose as I closed my eyes. I tried to hide the wince, but he saw it.

"Pretty deep for a nick."

"Just wrap it, Daniel."

He wiped the area dry and cleaned all around the wound. Then whipped the towel around my arm, folded it evenly, and tied a knot. It wasn't too tight, and the pressure was just right.

"You'll survive," he said.

"I've had worse."

"Why be so rough, Charolette? You can be gentle."

"I am what this world made me."

"Remember when—"

"Daniel. I don't wanna hear about what memories you think we've had. There's only one thing that needs to be comin' outta your damn mouth. Now tell me. Tell me about Jonah."

I appreciated what he had done. But there was no time. Soon these bullets wouldn't be hitting just arms. After my urging, he continued.

"I last saw him north of here." He looked me dead in the eyes. "In the Land of the Falcon Sky."

It was as if the whole world became quiet. "The Falcon Sky?"

"You say you don't believe in ghosts, Charolette, but I've seen 'em."

"You've been there?"

"That's where I found 'im."

"But no man comes back from there."

"No. They don't."

Stories. That's all they were. But I had to wonder, of all the things I'd heard, some of them must be rooted in truth. As the seed of the stories grew, where did the truth end and the nightmare begin?

"Have you ever seen the falcon?" I asked.

"I've seen it once."

"They say the falcon brings death."

"They do."

He spoke firmly, with a certainty that he would take to his grave. I needed him to have some doubt that the falcon was a messenger of death, but I searched his eyes and saw none. We were both lost in this moment and did not hear the creaking and cracks of the wood floorboards as someone emerged through the doorway.

The third person cleared his throat. It was our priest, Father Vincent, who knew us both when we were younger. An older man who helped settle this town before our time. He was moving carefully into the parlor, hands raised high, wearing a long black coat and his white collar. The second we saw the priest, Hennessy sprang toward the table and went for his gun.

"Hennessy!" I mirrored his burst forward and I met him at the table, grabbing the weapon at the same time as him. My one hand snatched the barrel and the other clung to his wrist, squeezing as tight as I could.

"Give it to me," Hennessy demanded.

"This wasn't the deal. Let go."

"You said no one was comin'."

The priest interjected, "Be careful there, you two."

Stunned that anyone else had dared to join me in here, I asked, "Father Vincent, what are you doing?"

"The Lord guided me here."

"I'd turn around if I were you," warned Hennessy.

"You don't have to do this, Hennessy," I said, still gripping the gun with all my might.

"He's here to kill me, just like the rest of 'em."

"That is not my intent."

"Never trust a Hennessy. Their words, not mine."

I told Hennessy, "He's a priest, for heaven's sake. Let go."

"I come armed only with the grace of God."

"God is not welcome here, priest."

"HEY. LET. GO," I threatened as my voice grounded deep and my breath began to hiss. I seemed to have gotten Hennessy's attention as his eyes snapped toward me. Then Father Vincent lifted the sides of his coat revealing no weapons at his hip. I felt Hennessy loosen his grip and let go of his weapon, and we both backed away from the table together. "Thank you, Daniel."

The priest asked, "Daniel, is it? Where's Jonah?"

"That's what I'm trying to find out," I said.

Father Vincent gave a warm, yet cautious look to Hennessy. "It's been a long time, Daniel. You're not a young man anymore."

"I'm not a lot of things."

"You were a good boy from a good family. I hate that all this has happened to you all."

"Oh, do you now?"

There was a tension between the two of them that I could not place. Even with Father Vincent, a feeling of uncertainty lingered. He was always such a kind man to all of us. A spiritual mentor and an advocate of peace in our town. Normally I'd welcome his presence here. But if Jonah was coming, we didn't need to complicate things further.

I asked again, "Father, why did you come?"

"Well, Charolette. I—"

"Sheriff."

He said after a slight hesitation, "Right." Then he gently nodded to me. "I'm here to keep everyone safe from harm."

"That's why *I'm* here," I tried to clarify.

"Then, I'm here to help."

"I'm gettin' along fine. I don't think there's more that you can do."

"You're fine? What happened to your arm?"

"Why don't you ask the men outside?"

Father Vincent looked to the bullet holes in the parlor and then to the blood-filled wrap on my arm. "Okay. I'll be here as the presence of God then."

Hennessy scoffed at that. Father Vincent turned to him with a gentle look, as he would to a child who needed guidance. "What's so funny?"

"Oh, nothin'. I'm just glad God could finally join us."

"God loves you, Daniel. He wants his lamb to return to the flock."

"Oh, yeah? He wants us all to come home?"

"We are all his children."

I tried to interject, "Father—"

"He wants *all* of us?" demanded Hennessy.

"We are all perfect in the eyes of God."

"The answer is supposed to be *yes*."

Father Vincent took a moment. I wasn't sure what point Hennessy was trying to make. He seemed to be trying to get under Father's skin. But Father Vincent didn't bite and instead just gently smiled and said, "Yes, Daniel. God wants us all to come home."

"Father Vincent, we're gonna leave this," I said. "Just let me speak with Daniel. He's gonna help us."

"How so?"

"Well . . . I don't know. We're gonna listen to him. He's promised that he can help us."

"Do we have time for that?"

"He's comin', Father."

Even him, the priest, the one who walked with the word of God on him, knew that that changed everything. That nothing was more dire than the possibility of the Nightmare's return.

"Okay. Whatever you think best, Charolette."

"Sher—. Oh, forget it." I brought my focus back to Hennessy, "Alright, Daniel. Tell me of the Falcon Sky."

"It ain't that easy."

"Oh," said the priest. "The Land of the Falcon Sky. Is that where Jonah is?"

"Yes," said Hennessy.

I asked, "What do you know about it, Father?"

"It's a place that I've never been. And you know well, Charolette, you and Hennessy both, that place is not to be reckoned with. You've heard the stories told when you were younger. The warnings as you all came of age. It's said to be a valley far north of here ending in two high, sharp ridges under a wide sky. Perfect home for a falcon. A lot of territory fighting happened up that way. Left everyone dead. A lot of graves. It's a cursed land now. A place of beauty, for sure. But a place of death. You won't find anything up there but savages and bandits now. If you go out there, you're going out there to die. And if those damn Indians don't get you, the wild will." Father Vincent then looked solely at me. As if what he said was somehow meant for me. "But the Falcon Sky is more than just a valley and a grave, Charolette. There be some troubled and lost souls say they have seen it without ever being there. For the falcon can haunt their minds from afar. Marking them with dreams of fire. And a message of death."

Of all the legends I had heard and things that seemed to stretch beyond reality, this one I believed most. It was greater than all this. The Land of the Falcon Sky had been around long before the Hennessys, and would remain when they were gone. Though, I would not concede that to them.

"But those are just stories," I said.

Then, I heard a slow faint drumming coming from somewhere inside the room. As Hennessy paced about the parlor, my eyes were drawn to the envelope that was still in his hand. The drumming grew louder. It seemed to me that the sound was coming from inside the envelope, beating and pulsing against its seal, like something was alive in there. But I shook my head free of it, looking back up to Hennessy, as the drumming faded away.

"Dreams of fire? Ain't sound like nothin' but the tales of drunk men," I told him.

"Let's hope you're right."

"Did Jonah's hunt take you there?"

Hennessy said, "It was bound to happen. We spent so much of our lives lookin' for that murderer."

"Strange that y'all spent so many years out there and never found him."

"Bad men are hard to kill."

"He needed to be tried."

"He needed to be judged by God," said the priest. "Not us. Not you, Hennessy."

"I saw men rob, steal, kill, in front of my own eyes."

I said, "That's not what I heard."

"That's not what I heard either," Father Vincent added.

"I was there," Hennessy objected.

Of the three of us, Hennessy was the only one there who had first-hand knowledge. He was there with Jonah when his wife took that bullet. But of all the other witnesses that were there that day, they all said the same thing. "I heard they were just there for gold and jewelry, and whatever they could find in people's pockets, not lookin' ta kill anyone," I said.

"That murderer shot Jonah's wife."

"Accidentally. And only in a struggle and in the chaos after Jonah tried to stop them."

"Should he have just let it happen?"

"Yes. And maybe his wife would still be alive."

"To hell with that."

"Those men weren't tryin' ta kill his wife, Daniel."

"Yeah, but one did. And I sat there next to Jonah as he held his wife. Grabbin' at air. Bleedin' out. Watchin' her gentle light fadin' away."

"That was honorable. Did y'all do the same for my husband?"

Hennessy's blank stare said it all. They hadn't. The Hennessys left my husband's body on the cold ground, lying in his own blood. Alone, save for God far above him and the dirt right beneath. He wasn't found for some time. They'd probably say they didn't have time, because they had to get out of there. Or maybe that they all had a path, and Crowley was just walking his. But neither story satisfied me. I found it barbaric to let a man die like that. To leave him to the wild. His body no longer recognizable. To not even let his friends see him again as he once was. It ruined me, seeing my husband lying there like that. It's something I could never unsee.

"Your husband . . . You're right. Jonah was wrong for what he did to Crowley. And we never should've left him there like that."

"You mean alone?"

"Yes."

"Left to the wild."

I could see Hennessy's guilt as he turned from my gaze and lowered his head. I wanted him to sit in that feeling for years, but he was quick to move on. "Why are you wearin' his badge?"

"Keep goin', Daniel," I urged.

He gave an agreeing nod. "In time, Jonah started to gather sort of a followin'. The more we rode, the darker it got. And the more that murderer's face began to blur. As time went on, the light in Jonah started ta die. He wasn't himself anymore."

"You mean after he started killin'."

"I love my brother, but, his eyes were . . . different."

The priest said, "The devil comes for us all. Your brother was not the first, and he won't be the last. But there's hope for Jonah still."

"No. There isn't."

"He can come to me, confess before the Lord our God, and he will be welcomed through the gates of Heaven."

"It's that easy, is it?"

"Our God is a merciful God."

"Forgiven? Just like that?"

"There is nothing that your brother could've done that would deny him salvation."

Hennessy's eyes homed in on Father Vincent. "You sure about that, priest?"

Father Vincent looked like a weight was just thrown on top of him, as he shifted back on his heels and his body seemed to be pulled a little into the floor. Like me, I bet he wondered about the actions of man that would have proved him wrong. I can't tell you anything about heaven or hell. But the thought of these unforgivable acts was terrifying. "How many do ya think?"

"I don't know, Charolette."

"Enough to be called the Nightmare?"

The Hennessys had been riding for years now. When pressed, Daniel couldn't recall for sure how many or even guess the number of deaths Jonah was responsible for. Time blurs and the days go by when you have a purpose. Something deep inside you that drives you to action. In their case, the hunt of a man. And all that does not serve that purpose gets lost in the abyss of your mind. Daniel said he wasn't proud of anything other than protecting his brother. He said Jonah's acts were a means to an end. How he tried to let himself be guided by his conscience, to be ruled by what he believed to be just. Regardless of how long the list might have been, he thought he was doing right by his brother. But I didn't buy it.

Hennessy said, "The first few encounters out there weren't at all like that. Killin' was rare, in the beginnin'."

"You could've come home. Before things turned."

"You'd think. But every town we rode into, every man we questioned, Jonah thought we were always getting closer. But the truth of it was, a man will tell ya just about anything with a bullet in his leg."

"I know ya think those men were all criminals. But do ya think he ever killed an innocent man?"

The priest said, "Thou shalt not kill, Charolette. It doesn't matter if he was innocent or not."

"In the eyes of the law it does," I argued.

"God is law."

I spoke over him. "Not for all of us, Father." This idea was where the priest and I parted. I turned back to Hennessy, "Do ya think he ever killed a man that didn't deserve ta die?"

"When ya ride with a particular group it says a lot."

"Should I judge *you* by the company you keep, Daniel? Your brother and his men sound just like the lot you're speakin' of. Is that a death sentence for you?" I took a strong step forward. "If so, why don't I put a bullet in you?"

I had truly meant it as a question rather than a threat, but my words came with a venomous bite. Hennessy shifted back on his heels at the words I cursed him with. It was just the hypocrisy of it all that was getting to me. But it caused the energy in the room to shift. We were now standing as if we had each hurried upon a snake in the wild.

I caught his eyes glancing at the table between us, and our focus went to the weapons that lay on top of it. There was nothing stopping either of us from rushing forward and ending this game that he was playing with me.

I surveyed the distance, calculating if I had gotten too far away or let him get too close. I looked up to him and wondered if he was thinking the same. *Would I make it in time?* Energy started to load in my legs, readying me to spring towards the gun if I needed to. I started to squint to keep myself from blinking.

A creak came from above us. I glanced up to see if anyone was at the railing or walking along the stairs. There was no one. It was still only the two of us caught up in this moment, with the thought of death focusing all of my senses. The feel of the sweat building on my forehead. The dry taste of cigar smoke and liquor still lingering in the air. The smell of burning torches coming in through the window. The sight of his frozen frame before me and the sound of my racing heart.

Father Vincent moved slowly between us. His voice remained soft and easeful, opening out his arms to us both. "Easy there. You two just take a breath now. Whatever it is you're thinking, just remember the person across from you is created in God's image. What you do to them, you're doing to God himself. Hennessy's got something to say, Charolette. Let's hear him out."

Hennessy watched the tension continue to build in me. How my shoulders were tightening and my hand was beginning to shake. I was ready to go for the gun, no matter the cost. In a few more breaths I would have done it. But Hennessy lifted his hands and floated back away from the table. His face was cool and calm. I didn't see any sign in him that he wanted to kill me. My hand went still and my shoulders rolled back. "Tell me what I need to hear, Daniel. This is your last chance."

He lifted the envelope and held it with two hands, staring at it as if he could see straight through to what was inside. I thought for a moment that the drumming had returned, but when I looked down to the mystery in Hennessy's hands, I heard nothing. He gazed up at me, continuing to circle away from the table.

"The man that you're looking for is gone. One night, a good while back, we were camped in the mountains near the edge of the Falcon Sky. It was one of those long days, at the end of a long week, and an even longer month. I watched Jonah stare into the fire, while the men around him got drunk or fell asleep. He was lost in the flames. Then, I heard this scream. A man's scream. And I saw from behind Jonah this massive grizzly step into the light. The entire camp scattered. Men waking up and crawling away for their lives. I yelled for Jonah, but just as he turned, the bear slashed his claws across Jonah's chest, hurling Jonah to the ground. I thought he was dead. But no. Jonah got ta his feet, pulled out his knife, and turned to face the grizzly. As if it was just another man. He said to the beast, 'No, sir. I don't think so.' I had never seen anything like it. He butchered that bear. And then he started cuttin' off its claws. Blood from the wound on his chest was fillin' his shirt, but he just kept cuttin', until he had every last one of 'em. He fashioned a necklace out of the claws and put them around his neck, then dipped his hands in the bear's blood and wiped it on his face and body. And just went back to staring into the fire. Everyday since, those claws have hung against his chest. So everyone knew who he was. The Nightmare. Jonah is gone. He's been reborn. He lives for only one thing now. Vengeance."

"Indeed," I whispered. To me, most of this was ridiculous. It was all becoming so absurd. *No man could kill a grizzly,* I thought. *Not with his bare hands.*

There's no way that thing wouldn't've just torn him apart. I just added it to the list of the many stories I refused to believe. But there was one thing I did recognize as true. *Vengeance.* It was a word I knew well and would not soon forget.

"He's only a man," I said.

"No, he ain't."

"Even so, my son. A grizzly is a . . . well, a grizzly," said Father Vincent.

"You don't believe me?"

"We're talking an animal that weighs upward of seven hundred pounds and could stand over eight feet tall."

"You strike me as the kind of man who believes in the unexplainable."

"I believe in miracles. Of the divine nature."

"Okay." I was willing to humor the idea. "Let's say it did happen."

Hennessy went on, "I think it was then that I knew I was gonna leave."

"That's when you came back?"

"The first time, yeah."

"This isn't your first time back?"

"No. I came a few months ago."

"I never seen ya."

"I slipped in at night. I wasn't here long. Just long enough to see what y'all had done."

"What?"

Trying to change the subject, the priest said, "I'm more concerned with where Jonah is now."

"Done to who, Daniel?"

"No one did anything to anyone, Charolette."

Hennessy turned to the priest. "Should I tell her or should you?"

"The Hennessys lost their faith a long time ago. Their absence from the church is something I've noticed for many years."

"Faith isn't only found within the walls of your house."

"It isn't my house. It's your father's house. Your savior's house. And leaving that, it's no wonder y'all were led astray."

Hennessy's voice dropped. "Bring God into it one more time."

"Easy, Daniel," I warned.

"You're a wounded man, I can see that. If you'd just—" Saying this, Father Vincent took a step toward Hennessy, which also happened to be toward the guns on the table. Hennessy was quick to get just one step closer, not knowing Father's intentions.

"You watch it, priest."

Father Vincent crept back away from the table. "You know I mean you no harm. Hennessy, these weapons are nothing to me. They're nothing compared to his power. I want to help you."

The looks Hennessy had been giving Father Vincent since he had entered the parlor could've pierced iron. Something wasn't right. "Daniel, look at me. Did to who?"

"Why did you put that badge on if you're not going to do anything?"

"I don't know what you're talkin' about."

"Don't lie ta me."

"I ain't lyin'."

"The rest of my family. Tell me, Charolette, what did they ever do?"

Hennessy's other brothers and parents were left behind when Jonah and Daniel had gone. The Hennessys were one of the more well known and well liked families about the town before recent years. A family that many people went to when they needed help, and the Hennessy boys were called upon often. A broken fence out on a ranch, a wagon stuck in the mud, they were always eager to oblige.

But after the death of Jonah's wife and as time went on and the stories of Jonah and Daniel's journey reached home, most believed their quest for justice turned into something far more deadly. More time passed and with it came more stories, leading many to assume that the Hennessys' inability to find what they were looking for had driven them mad, that they were hungry for blood, no longer able to see reason. Fear spread throughout the town and people had become wary of the rest of his brothers as well. Some held the whole family responsible, while others simply worried about crossing their paths and about what might happen to them if they did. I didn't see the rest of the family much. They kept to themselves, ever since the boys had gone.

"You know, my father's not for much these days. You see, he was always worried about us. Always hopin' we'd come home. He heard some of Jonah's followers had come ridin' through. Found himself one night back again in this very parlor. Hopin' to ask them if they had seen us. He walked right through those doors. But Jonah's men weren't here. It was only the men of this town. Just a man lookin' for his sons and bunch of local drunks. They beat 'im and whipped 'im somethin' good. Just because he was a Hennessy. We don't know if he'll make it. Just a waitin' game now."

"If that did happen, I don't know how you can blame this whole town for it."

"You mean beatin' him to near certain death? Oh, I don't blame all y'all for that. No. I blame the rest of y'all for watchin' it happen. His body laid on the floor right here. I blame those that stood over him and mocked him. I blame those who left him there for dead, for my family to find him there the next mornin', barely alive." His voice went hard as Hennessy turned to look at Father Vincent. "I blame the priest who was in this parlor. The priest who let his flock spit on my father's beaten body, lying there cold and still. That's who I blame."

"What? Is this true, Father?"

"It is not, Charolette," replied the priest.

"You stood over him and watched him bleed. You're a goddamn liar."

"I am not, Daniel. I was not here. But there is some truth to his story, Charolette. The devil is everywhere. We are all sinners. I heard that his father was left there. And I didn't come. I thought it was the best—"

"Christ, Father. Why?" I asked.

Father Vincent was struggling to find an answer. "There was . . . a lot to consider."

"He's an old man, Father. He helped build this town with you." Father Vincent looked down and away from me. He knew what part he had to play in all this. I looked over to Hennessy who didn't blink. His eyes were fixed on Father Vincent. But maybe he wasn't the only guilty one. Like the rest of the town, I watched as a shadow was cast over all of the Hennessys. Glancing down at the badge, thinking how consumed I'd been since putting it on, I began to wonder if I, too, was a part of it all. What the town had become. "That was never brought to my attention, Daniel."

"Where has your mind been, Charolette? Obviously not here."

"I'm sorry."

"Hey, let's not you and me start tossin' empty apologies around. You can see it though, right? My father's body lyin' there. Blood drainin' out of him. Picture it. Right here. Leavin' 'im ta die. Alone. I reckon you know a thing or two about that."

Hennessy's family had been fading out of mind and moving toward early graves. Hearing these stories made my blood catch fire as my heartbeat increased. I was tired of seeing people destroyed by all this. For the first time I began to wonder if it wasn't just the Nightmare. That maybe as Jonah faded from the light, we too followed close behind. *I'm not like him*, I thought. The vision of confronting the Nightmare came to me often. Sometimes during the day, always at night. And as the scene played out in my mind, I just stood there across from a dark silhouette surrounded by a hot glow. I would try so hard to lift the gun I carried, but I couldn't. My body always frozen, never able to breathe. *With every part of my being, I'd do it. I'd kill Jonah for what he's done.* I saw that vision again then and wondered if I was becoming as black as that which came to me at night. If I, too, was fading like the rest of them. But it pained me to hear of Hennessy's father, and that compassion was hope for me. That if indeed I was following behind the Nightmare, I was not completely like him yet.

The priest asked Daniel, "Why don't you all let me come to him, your father?"

"No, it's too late for that."

"I was wrong, Hennessy. I should've come. Repentance has been a daily task for me. God has brought me to this moment, presented me with the opportunity to right a wrong. I can bless your father. Pray over him, in case the worst should come to pass."

I said, "No, Father, I think you've done enough." I looked up to the mirror with the bullet holes in it, and it was now my face that I saw, the shattered bits filling one side of it. I couldn't quite tell what it was I saw in there. It was as if I could no longer recognize the person looking back at me. I asked myself, "How could I not know?"

"You ain't here," Hennessy said. "You took up Crowley's iron. You put on that badge. But you're gone."

"I didn't want to put it on."

"Then why did ya?"

"Someone has to do something."

"But that someone didn't have to be you."

The priest said, "Now, I'm gonna have to agree with you there, Hennessy. I didn't think it was the best idea either. It doesn't help much having a woman walking around town trying to be a sheriff."

"Well, Father, no one else would."

"I don't believe that," Hennessy stated.

"It's the truth."

"No one?"

The priest offered his opinion. "There weren't many candidates to choose from."

"There was no one. Not one man thought it was worth the risk, standin' for my husband."

"Why?"

Again the priest tried to answer, "Well, there are a lot of men in this town in positions of great importance. We need those men to stay in—"

"The Nightmare."

Father Vincent said nothing this time. And his silence confirmed I was right. Hennessy looked at me for a moment, like he knew what I was going to say but still wanted me to say it.

"Tell me."

"They thought he'd be out for 'em. This whole town has been livin' in an ever-growin' darkness. And as the nights have gone by, I have sat. Waitin'. And each day is just like the last. I see it. I see the end. I'm stuck in the world of . . . . They talk of him like he's a ghost. They say he looks like death walkin'. That he stands close to the fire ta watch things burn. He rides a horse black as coal. That he waits for ya at night. When ya can't see him. Some say that he can't be killed. But they know he's comin'. He's comin' for all of us."

"That what you think?" asked Hennessy.

The priest said, "I think there are forces that can't be explained. But they are all the work of the Lord our—"

"I wasn't talkin' to you."

I wondered about this often. What are the chances that everyone was wrong? What could be another possibility? Maybe I was just trying to think of something that would make me less terrified. The thing I told myself to push me through that parlor door knowing the Nightmare might be inside.

"Me?" I thought for a moment. "No." I came back from my thoughts to Daniel's question. "I don't believe that. I think he's scared. Just a scared little boy in a man's body who can't find his way home." I tried to stand tall when I said it. To hold my ground. Though I wasn't entirely sure how to do that. I doubted what I said the second it came out of my mouth. The truth was, I wondered if the star on my chest was just a target for the Nightmare. So he knew where to find my heart.

Hennessy moved across the room closer to me, easing his way forward. He sat down on one of the parlor chairs in front of me, placing the envelope on the floor beside him. It was silent at that moment. I was still thinking of Jonah and the stories that had immortalized him. I think we all were.

Then from inside my mind came a cluster of cries. I brought my hands to my ears, as if that would make them stop. Along came the flames, followed by the silhouettes of unknown women trapped in fire. I shook my head and pushed it all down, and then looked back to Hennessy. Somehow, the room seemed to get darker. The fear started to make my blood move faster, my body growing tense. I couldn't allow myself not to trust my instincts when thinking of the Nightmare. I had to be sure of myself. I began to pace in front of the two others in this room.

"Nightmare or not, it doesn't change the fact of what y'all've done."

"You shouldn't be here," Hennessy said.

"Don't patronize me."

"I mean no disrespect."

"I'm here to do right by my husband and those poor souls your brother took."

"Mostly criminals."

"Men, Hennessy," I corrected him. "Call them criminals, call them bandits, call them whatever the hell you like. They were men. Men with families. With fathers and brothers. And it wasn't just them, was it? There's always more, isn't there? What about the women y'all came across out there?"

Hennessy took a deep breath and looked to the ground, letting out a hard sigh. When he looked back at me, his eyes had changed. It felt as if the ground had rumbled. I didn't recognize him anymore. A fire began to spin inside Hennessy, "I don't know what you've heard—"

"Tell me about all the women that deserved to be taken."

"Those stories aren't true."

"Which is it, Daniel? Is it wrong or not? Is Jonah somehow different? You Hennessys are all the same. Ya look out for your own, no matter the cost. Including innocent women."

"That never happened!"

Hennessy exploded to his feet causing me to lunge for the table. It happened quicker than I think we both expected. Before he could reach me, I grabbed the nearest gun and pointed it at him. I held it with two hands to try to stop my shaking. Hennessy could see the barrel aimed straight for his heart. A sight that didn't seem unfamiliar to him as he barely flinched. It's said that killers always aim for the heart. But I wasn't a killer like them. Although I guess that'd be decided for sure when I'd finally meet the Nightmare. For now, I just needed him to believe I could be.

"Y'all deserve to die for doin' that."

"You don't know what you're talkin' about."

"Y'all aren't men. You're somethin' else."

"Stories, Charolette. Stories."

"Not all of them."

"You can't pick and choose which ones to believe," Hennessy said.

I didn't respond. I let the iron talk for me. Hennessy turned to Father Vincent. "Stand in front of me, priest."

Father Vincent turned to address me but did not intervene as Hennessy had asked. "Now, Charolette."

"Stand in front of me," repeated Hennessy.

"She's not going to do what everyone's been telling her to do."

"She's got that iron on me, damn it. Stand in front of me. She won't harm a priest."

"Everything is going to be—"

"GET BETWEEN US."

"I do not govern the lives of others, Hennessy," the priest declared. "Nor will I throw myself in the middle of a decision that was created for this woman and this woman alone. Our Lord is watching. She has a choice to make. She will make it, and she will live by it."

Father Vincent walked over and stood next to me, even slightly behind me, as if to whisper in my ear. "Search your heart, child. You know what you need to do. There is a reason you are here. Accept what you know to be true. Look at this man. Does he look like one who deserves death?"

I looked deep into Hennessy. There was so much pain in him. "I don't know, Father." Then

Hennessy closed his eyes for a moment, and when he opened them again, the fire that had started behind them was gone. I saw him again. The fear left me and a familiar sense returned.

Hennessy said, "Alright. Yeah. My brother is a killer. There were people that didn't deserve ta die. He's tryin' ta do right by his wife. I will not judge him for that. You can go and do that yourself. And you have every right, wantin' ta honor your husband. If you wanna think ya need justice for him and those poor bastards, go right ahead. But do not—DO NOT—say this is for any woman who ya heard been done wrong. That never happened. Not once. I can't speak for the other men he rode with or the people that followed him. But I can speak for me, and I can speak for Jonah. The road was one thing. And one thing only. And I'll stop calling it justice. Since we both know it went beyond that. But never women."

The Hennessys were never like that from what I remembered. Though not all men are what they seem. I had heard that story too many times and found it hard to believe, though as the tales of the Hennessys took on a life of their own, maybe this was just another part that had manifested in the nightmares of others. But the more I talked with Daniel, as each moment passed by, the Hennessy before me became less and less what I thought I'd see. Even though it might have been hard to find, what bits of compassion I did discover in him had to count for something. And this was the most I had talked with another person for some time.

"I'll take that with what little comfort it brings," I said.

"Charolette, I don't think you understand the world you're in."

"I understand well enough."

"This isn't you. You don't have the eyes for it."

"I see just fine."

"You want to be a killer, Charolette? Sadly, you need to be. You need to be the kind of person that would've pulled that trigger already."

"I don't believe that."

"And that's what's gonna get ya. Listen, promise me—"

"You're far away from promises, Daniel."

"When this is done, when I finish what I have to say, you'll quit."

"I ain't stoppin'."

"There are bad men out there."

"And right in front of me."

"Men worse than me. You're gonna get hurt. Wearin' your husband's badge. Carryin' his iron. Have you ever even shot that thing before? People who don't know that won't look kindly on ya. They'll think ya know what you're doin', and they will kill you."

The list of people who thought I couldn't be the sheriff we needed was long. And being talked to like a child was a regular occurrence. I already had a hard enough time trying to convince *myself* I was up to the task. But Hennessy's concerns seemed genuine and weren't coming from a place of malice. I could see that he was trying to look out for me. I had forgotten what it felt like to have someone worry.

I thought back to the time I met Daniel, by the creek when we were young. He was so handsome to me. He still was, even with the tattered clothes and his sun-beaten face. But again, I just let those feelings pass through me, and I returned to where I needed to be.

"I'll put his badge down once my husband can rest." I walked back toward the table, put the gun back down, and stepped away. "Now what's in that envelope?"

"You're right. It's time." Hennessy reached down to pick up the envelope. "I wish my brother hadn't led me here."

"Is he coming to kill us?" I asked.

"You know . . . I can feel him," Hennessy said.

"How long do we have?"

"He's already here."

It was as if all the breath in my body had been pulled out of me. My muscles went tight and my joints began to lock and I became like stone. Then, of course, the fire returned. And the whisper followed. My time with the Nightmare was near. I had to break free of the spell. My jaw slowly started to move, and then air finally poured back in. I needed to remain calm. We all did.

But that wasn't easy for the priest as he gasped, "Oh, hell, Lord God, Jesus."

I slowly turned to look at Father Vincent, who had proved again how fast the fear sinks in. How quick it was for some men to act contrary to what they had been preaching. And I was the one they patronized? I reminded him, "Careful, Father. The Lord's name."

"Yes. Of course. Sorry."

I turned back to Hennessy. "Do you believe he can be killed?"

"He can," Hennessy said. He walked toward me and tossed the envelope on the table. It landed like a brick, solid and firm, with a clap that made me jump. I reached for it. It felt heavy to me. I ran my fingers along the seal. I opened it and looked inside. I blinked a few times, confused and not knowing what to make of it.

"I don't understand," I said.

"Do you talk with ghosts, Charolette?"

"What?"

"Do the dead speak to you?"

"No. I don't know what you're talking about."

"I believe Jonah spoke to the dead. I think they were guidin' him. He was—"

"A monster."

Hennessy nodded. Not in agreement. Almost as a confirmation that he knew I'd continue saying things like that. "After I found out what happened to our father, I thought that I could reach Jonah. That if I could go back to him and let him know what was happening to his family, that he'd see. That I could pull him out of there."

"The Land of the Falcon Sky."

"It's worse than what we were told as kids, you know? God, it's so quiet up there. You don't even hear the animals. Except for the falcon when it comes. The terrain is hard. But the real danger is the kind of men roamin' that far north. Men of the wild. Scavengers and bandits. And of course the Indians. That land is sacred to them. And with losin' so much already, they'd do anything to protect it. They found Jonah travelin' out there."

"Did they try to kill him?"

"No. They let him through. They watched as he passed by them with those claws hangin' around his neck. It's where he got his name."

"The Nightmare?" I asked.

"They called him Napusai Pitsih. The Nightmare."

"They feared him?"

"Everyone fears him. But I think they understood what he had become." Hennessy wasn't looking at me anymore. His gaze had drifted out into the parlor, and suddenly I could see he was no longer there with me. He was back in the Land of the Falcon Sky. "It wasn't so easy for *me*. The Indians found me. They didn't kill me, but they didn't let me through either. They put me on the ground and sat around me for some time. I think they saw Jonah in me. Hell, by the looks of me, they might have even thought I was him at first. Then they started tappin' their chests." Hennessy slapped the palm of his hand to his heart a few times, and then again with his fist. "They could see my heart, like they saw his. They knew why I was there. And they let me through."

"Why were you there?" I asked.

"Despite everything, it's a beautiful land. Jonah's camp overlooked the valley. I found him at the top of the ridge during sunset, lyin' back watchin' the night fall. His eyes never blinked. I told him what happened to our father, that he needed to come home. That he needed to make it right. And he'd be goin' back one way or another."

I reached into the envelope. When I gripped its contents I could feel the tips of a few long blades. My hand emerged from the envelope holding a necklace. And on it hung the sharp claws of a grizzly. Woven between the daggers were a few feathers, tattered and matted. But their colors were still bright, making the blackness of the claws like the pitch of night. Hennessy's voice began to shake. He rubbed his neck and paced back and forth in front of me. I sat down in one of the chairs and held the necklace in my lap. The faint drumming returned, and with it, that flash of fire.

He went on, "God damn, the gun was so heavy. I had ta think about my family. As a whole. I just wanted things ta go back ta the way they were. I wanted him ta walk down with me." There was a pause in Hennessy as he froze, staring at something or someone back out under the Falcon Sky. And then, "I put a bullet in his heart. Three of 'em. Ta make sure there was nothin' left of what was already gone."

No. No. I couldn't believe it. My eyes were fixed on the claws. *It can't be*, I thought. Then, like in my dreams, I tried to move but couldn't. I was trying to breathe but it was as if my throat was blocked. My vision went dark, and I saw again a horizon in flames. I squeezed my eyes shut as the inferno consumed my mind. Then the cries of all those he took screamed out from the flames and in my heart. I held the claws to my chest, opened my eyes, and finally breathed.

"Jonah's dead?"

"I wish it had been me," Hennessy said.

"You killed your brother?"

"My brother has been gone a long time. It was just the end of the Nightmare."

Father Vincent moved in closer to me, eyeing the necklace in my hand. "These belonged to the Nightmare? The claws of that grizzly?"

"That's them," said Hennessy.

"Where is his body?" I asked.

"With the worms."

Father Vincent reached out his hand and asked me, "May I?" I handed him the claws, and he took them gently away from me and gazed on them like they were an ancient relic.

"He's gone?" I asked myself.

"I'm sorry."

"For what? Hennessy's dead."

"I know it's not how you wanted it. I know you wanted your own kind of justice."

"He's gone," I said it again. Almost as if to convince myself it was so. But something didn't feel right. My stomach was spinning. Was this the kind of reckoning I had hoped for?

"So, ya see. I needed you ta know. I needed all the people out there ta know, it's over. He can't hurt anyone anymore. I'm sorry. My family is sorry. We just want things ta go back to the way they were."

"I don't think it's that easy."

I was trying to make sense of it all. My whole world, and everything that brought me here, was now spinning. I questioned if this was going to be acceptable. I thought that this might not be enough to satisfy them. I didn't know if I was satisfied. The list of crimes was long. And it couldn't have all been just Jonah.

"But I gave you what ya wanted," Hennessy said.

"I didn't want this."

"You didn't?"

"It didn't have to happen like this."

"This was the only way."

"What about all that you've done?"

"What do ya mean?"

"How many men have you killed, Daniel? When you were ridin' with him, how many times did you watch it happen?"

"It's not the same."

"Did you watch? Or did you pull the trigger?"

"I never went too far. I didn't become like him. I never killed a man who wasn't tryin' to kill me. And that's the truth."

I searched his eyes. He couldn't see it. "Except your brother."

Hennessy didn't respond. He just closed his eyes and lowered his head, as if his spirit had left his body for a moment. Then he collapsed down in the chair opposite me. "What is it gonna take? What the hell do we need to do to make this right? Tell me. Tell me what to do, and I'll do it. I just want my family safe. There are dead-or-alive signs all over this goddamn town with Jonah's face on 'em. And you know y'all been wantin'im dead. You all have. I've brought ya that. I gave ya what you've all been beggin' for. And it comes at a price. A price that none of ya will ever have to pay. That's on me. That'll come for me on my judgment day. I'll admit I'm not proud about how all this played out. But just like you sought justice for your husband, I sought the same for Jonah. I would've done the same for you if you'd asked me. If you were my kin I would have rode witcha. I would have hunted them down and cursed those who chose not to help or who hindered our cause. Day and night, I would've been witcha. And I never would've stopped until you told me to. We all wanted this to end. I ended it. Now you need to do what's right. My brother is dead. I killed him. I buried him in the Land of the Falcon Sky. And when I die, it'll be that which I remember. Now, please, do what's right."

What's right, I thought. I wished I knew what that was. It sounded nice to me, having someone by my side in all this, pushing through the unknown. It would've been welcome company. With the Nightmare gone, there was no need for me to wear that star anymore. No reason for either of us to endure more trials. The weight that Hennessy would now have to carry I thought would be impossible for most. The thought of what he had done would never leave his mind. It would always be there. I wouldn't wish having to bear what he had done to his brother on anyone. I studied Hennessy, looking for the signs I thought I'd see. One of those Hennessys made of ash and smoke. Men without fear or remorse. Those who knew no pain. But all I saw was sorrow stretched across his face. He looked tired. I knew what it meant to be tired.

Father Vincent walked back to us, still admiring the claws. "Thank you for telling us all this, Hennessy." He handed the necklace back to me. "This is a gargantuan weight you have carried. The Lord has tasked you greatly."

I agreed with Father Vincent, "I'm sorry. That's not something anyone should have to bear. I want this done with, too. It's just so hard to imagine."

"It's been a long time."

"It has," the priest added.

"Too long." I wiped my hands over my face. "Okay. This all needs to be over. It's time."

"Thank you," said Hennessy.

"Let me just think for a second."

"Thank you, Charolette."

My stomach was beginning to turn, and I leaned forward with my forearms on my thighs. "Oh, god." I rocked back and forth taking a few deep breaths. Sitting back up I brushed my fingers over the badge. "I thought I might die wearing this thing. It was hard not givin' in to the stories sometimes."

"It's okay, Charolette."

I held up the bear claws, staring at their curved, dagger-like tips. My fingers weren't even as long. I dragged the claws across my chest, imagining what it would have felt like to have them dig into my skin and tear open my flesh. Like it did his. My breath quivered, and I threw the claws back to my lap. "He killed a grizzly?"

"Yeah."

"With his bare hands?"

"And a knife."

"Jesus Christ."

"Quite difficult to imagine," said the priest. "But remarkable."

"Oh my god. He's gone."

Hennessy tried to assure me. "He's gone."

My breathing became faster. "He's gone," and faster, "He's gone," and faster, "He's gone." I could feel the blood drain from my face. I sprang up, knocked the bottles off the nearby bar, leaned over the edge, and threw up. I hung my head there for a moment until I turned around and slid down the side of the bar, knocking over a couple of stools. A few breaths later, I was calm again.

"Jonah's spirit lives under the Falcon Sky now. You don't have to worry anymore."

There was guilt in knowing my chance to kill the Nightmare was gone. I couldn't look at either of them. My head fell back against the bar, and I closed my eyes. "Did he say anything before he died?" I asked.

"Like what?"

"Was he . . . sorry?"

"I think he saw the grizzly again."

"How so?"

"All he said was, 'No sir, I don't think so.'"

Out of nowhere came a violent flurry of bullets as the men outside fired a sudden burst of rounds. I shielded myself as bottles exploded on the bar above my head. The smell of bourbon filled the air as it dripped down around me. Hennessy and

Father Vincent dove to the floor for cover, holding their arms over their heads to shield themselves. The shots trailed off, and it was silent again.

"I swear. You see, Father? They're afraid of a dead man," I said.

Hennessy said, "They're not gonna stop."

"They're just doing what they believe God wants."

"I need to go out there and talk to them." I picked myself up from under the bar and dusted off pieces of the broken bottles. I crept towards the front of the parlor to get a look out from the edge of the window, trying to spy on all those waiting, gauging how far they were from the door, counting the number of barrels I could see. Hennessy moved to the window as well, standing on the opposite side.

Still taking cover, the priest said, "Talk to them? Out there? That doesn't sound wise."

"I'll tell them about Jonah. That he's gone."

"Do you think they'll believe you?" asked Hennessy.

"I agree with Hennessy, I don't see them listening to—"

"If they know he's gone, they might stand down and we can talk civilized," I interrupted.

"Like how you gonna do it though?" Hennessy asked.

"I don't know. Just step out there and say, 'The Nightmare is dead.'"

"You're just gonna do it like that, huh?"

"I don't know, maybe. I'm open to suggestions."

The priest said, "I suggest you don't do it."

"What do you propose then?"

"Let Hennessy go."

"They'll kill him."

"You can barely stand in front of that window. You think they'll be shy when the door opens? They could kill you just as easily."

"We can talk our way out of this."

Hennessy disagreed, "I think we're beyond that now."

"But wasn't this the whole point?"

"That was before I knew they'd be sendin' blind bullets into a buildin' with an innocent woman and a priest in it."

"You're right. I'm a woman wearin' her husband's badge, so they don't trust me. As long as they get Hennessy. But you're not just gonna ride out of here."

"Walkin' out is a death sentence. By bullet or rope."

Just beyond the window I caught sight of a reward poster. One with a dark sketch of the Nightmare. And below it had the words *or Alive* scratched through. Only the word *Dead* remained. No, Daniel wasn't the Hennessy whose picture was scattered throughout the town. But he did ride with Jonah and he was his brother. There was no way I could tell how'd they'd react to Jonah being gone, and how much more blood they'd demand. I believed Daniel had paid his price because of what he did to Jonah. The rest might not see it like that. Regardless, I knew my talking with them was the only way.

Hennessy looked at me for a moment like he was trying to see if I was lying, searching my face for some tell. But it didn't seem like he found what he was looking for. Then he nodded his head to me. Hennessy was closer now to where he had hoped to be. But it was going to take one more step. It was going to be difficult to convince all those men out there. But the way he now looked at me was different. Like I had become more familiar to him. I'm not sure what it was, but he seemed hopeful.

Hennessy leaned in toward me. "You think you can get 'em ta listen?"

"You got me to," I said.

On the verge of smiling, he teased me with, "But you're a woman."

"Yeah. I keep hearing that." I turned away from him and toward the table with our weapons. "I should get my gun."

"You should probably leave that," the priest suggested.

"Yeah?"

"You want to walk out there holding a weapon?"

Hennessy agreed. "He's right."

"Okay. Let me get the necklace."

I grabbed the claws buried in pieces of glass on the floor. The faint sound of drumming returned. It grew louder and louder. The claws felt so alive in my hand. I could feel them pulsing, a heart beating in them. That slow drumming pulled my gaze deeper into their long, rigid curves.

Hennessy watched me from a distance until he finally said, "Charolette?" The drumming came to a sharp end as I woke from the trance. "You okay?"

I whipped around. "Yeah." I started to make my way toward the parlor door.

The priest said, "I really don't think this is a good idea."

"Thank you for your concern, Father," I said.

Hennessy reached out and placed his hand softly on my arm, as if suggesting he would hold me back. "You don't have to do this."

"Yeah, I do." I brushed by him. I didn't move quickly. In fact, I was inching my way, bit by bit. It was now more quiet than it had ever been. The glass crunched beneath my feet. I could hear the roaring of the torches through the broken windows. I could hear the two of them breathing near me. Then it became surprisingly steady for me. I scoffed and smiled as I kept my eyes forward. I caught a quick glimpse into a life that I was no longer living. Back when Daniel and I were younger. I longed for that world. The innocence. For a time before all of this started. When nightmares didn't keep me awake. What he did back then, it did mean something to me. I was thankful to him for that memory. I turned back to Hennessy. "Oh, I hate licorice."

"What?"

"When we were young. The licorice you gave me. I hated it."

"Well, if we make it out of this alive, we'll have to find you something that you do like."

"Yeah, we'll see."

I gave a smirk and as I began to feel the blood rush to my face, I looked away. I then noticed that I hadn't moved. My inching toward the door had stopped long ago, and I was just standing in the middle of the parlor. I got to moving again. *I'll keep him alive*, I thought. An affection for him was building, a thought that was emerging in the back of my mind. All it would take to put an end to me or him was one rogue bullet. Just one man out there too spooked by the sight of Hennessy. A slip of an inch.

"WAIT," yelled the priest.

I stopped just before reaching the door and turned back to Father Vincent. He held his hand out reaching for me, while his head turned toward the window, his eyes peering out into the darkness. "What?" I asked.

"Something doesn't feel right."

"None of this does, Father."

"How do we know he isn't lying?"

"He's not lyin'."

"But if he is. It could be a trap. The Nightmare could be out there. Still alive. Waiting for this moment."

Hennessy said, "No one's waitin'."

Father Vincent came close to me and lowered his voice. "Charolette, he's a Hennessy. You have to think about the men outside. They have families."

But Hennessy could still hear him. "*I* have a family."

"That's not enough."

There came that doubt creeping back in again. Being scared to make the wrong decision. I turned to Hennessy to confirm, "Daniel, is someone waitin'?"

"No."

"Are you lyin'?"

"No."

Father Vincent moved toward the center of the parlor and cleared the area of chairs. "There's only one way we can tell that."

"How's that possible?" I asked.

He gestured to the floor before his feet, offering it up to Hennessy. "Kneel here, on the floor, before God, Hennessy. Let's have you confess."

"There will be no kneeling from me," said Hennessy.

"Let me hear your confession. And swear before God."

"No."

"I'll take your apprehension as a sign of guilt."

"I have nothing to say to you or your God."

"Does that comfort you, Charolette?"

"If he wanted to hide something, he would just lie ta ya," I said.

"Do not underestimate what a man will do when faced with certain death. One does not simply lie to God in the moment before he might die. Even those of little faith. Because even though it's little, that tiny piece of them wonders if they're wrong."

"I'm not doin' it."

"I leave it to you, Charolette. It's your life. You're the one walking through that door."

The two men looked at me, each waiting for me to agree with him. I hadn't talked to God in a while. Hadn't had much need to of late. My mind was visited by enough already. But it did remind me of our life before this. I'd much rather be there than here. I looked to Hennessy. "It wouldn't hurt, Daniel."

"Charolette—"

"Just do it," I said.

"This is a waste of time."

The priest said, "Is time all of a sudden important to you? It will only take a moment."

"It'll put me at ease," I told him.

Hennessy wiped his hands over his face and gave in to our request. "Okay, priest. I'll confess."

"Good. Come to me and to your Lord. Kneel." I could see Hennessy didn't like being commanded. He loosened his jaw and his shoulders and came to the center of the parlor. Father Vincent pulled out a rosary from his pocket and put it around his neck. He then placed his hand on Hennessy's back as Hennessy knelt down in front of him. With his other hand, Father made the sign of the cross and then held his palm out, open above Hennessy. "You are now in the presence of the almighty savior, the Lord Jesus Christ, and the Holy Ghost. You will begin, 'Forgive me, oh Lord, for I have sinned.'"

"Forgive me, Lord. For I have sinned."

"Yes, you have, Hennessy. My sheep. I am here to welcome you back to the flock. I'm listening."

"Don't you know my sins, Lord?"

"I do. But I need you to tell them to me. It is the act of reconciliation. You must confess to me or my gates will not open to you so that you may enter the kingdom of heaven."

"Okay. I've been . . . hurtful."

You could tell by Hennessy's frustrated tone he wasn't taking any of this seriously. But Father Vincent remained upright and still, and was not discouraged by it as he kept his eyes closed and his palm still open above Hennessy's head. He patiently waited like he would have done with a small child talking to God for the first time. "I'm still listening, my son."

Hennessy reluctantly continued, "I have dishonored my father."

"Yes."

"I have dishonored my mother."

"You did. How?"

"This is ridiculous."

"No, Hennessy. You say that you have dishonored your mother and your father. Well, you can honor them now. And you might not believe in my voice, in the tongue of Jehovah, in the one who sparked life in you. None of that matters. But what waits for you on the other side of that door could either send you to meet your creator or to oblivion.

This might be your last moment. Honor your family and the life you have had. Confess."

I was beginning to think that this was good for Hennessy. Not that I thought he was lying, but for him to get to ask for forgiveness before what might be the end for us all. But Hennessy did nothing. He knelt in silence. Unmoved. Then Father Vincent looked over to me.

"Come here, child." He waved for me to come next to him.

He put his hand on my shoulder and guided me down to the floor to kneel in front of Hennessy. As those eyes of his gazed upon me, I only saw the boy that I once knew. It felt safe kneeling with him. Father Vincent was standing above the two of us.

He let the moment settle with us, and then said, "If not to God, then to her, Hennessy. Confess before her. Let her be your chronicle. Let her carry your story."

Hennessy would've up and left. To him it was nothing but a charade. But he stayed looking at me. I didn't believe he did it for his brother. Or the other ones he was trying to protect. He definitely didn't do it for Father. Looking at him then, I believe he did it for me.

"I failed my family."

"I can't hear you, my son."

"I failed my family," Hennessy said louder.

"Go on."

"I abandoned them. I left them alone."

"On a quest for blood."

"Yes, Lord."

"What else?"

"I took the Lord's name in vain. I have stolen. I have coveted my neighbor's goods. His wife."

"I hear your sins. But we must hear them all."

Hennessy hesitated. He looked up to the priest and then back to me. But he didn't stay there long, as he turned his eyes from my view and lowered his head. "I . . . I have killed."

"We know, my son. What were their names?"

"I don't know, my Lord."

"How many?"

"I don't know, my Lord."

"Your Lord forgives you. There is still one thing left to confess, isn't there?"

"Yes."

"Yes," said the priest, as if he finally found what he was looking for. "Tell us, and be welcomed to the life everlasting."

"I am guilty of bearin' false witness."

"You have lied, Hennessy."

"Yes, my Lord."

"What is your most recent lie?"

"About my brother."

You could hear in Father Vincent's voice he was getting eager. He was getting closer to proving what he believed was true. "Yes. What about him?"

"I didn't kill him."

"So, he is alive?"

"No. He's dead."

Father Vincent paused. He was confused. This was not what he expected Hennessy to say. "Then who killed him?"

"The Nightmare."

"I see. So, you *are* here alone?"

"Yes."

"Are these the claws of the Nightmare?"

"Yes."

Father Vincent knelt down next to Hennessy. He put his hand over his heart like he was trying to protect it. Then he asked one last thing to save him from eternal damnation. "Swear to me, Hennessy. Before me, the Lord your God, and this woman, whose life you have in your hands, is there anyone waiting outside?"

Hennessy lifted his head back up and looked straight into my eyes. "No."

A great sigh of relief came from Father Vincent as he stood back up. He placed his hand gently on the back of Hennessy's head. "I release you from this burden you have carried, my son. I have washed your sins away. Be humbled before God and bow your head. Receive your penance." He reached out to me as well. "You too, Charolette." I caught one last glimpse of Hennessy's eyes as

Father Vincent guided us to bow our heads before him and before God.

"Close your eyes. You will say the Lord's prayer. You will go forth to honor your family and respect your neighbors. I forgive you, my son."

There was a peace in kneeling. Even as I bowed my head. Though, when I closed my eyes the flashes came as they always did. Fire and flames. And I don't know if it was because I was fighting the images again or if it was the fact that he moved ever so carefully, but I didn't hear Father Vincent as he moved away from us and toward the table. The table with Hennessy's gun. He quietly grabbed the weapon, crept back toward us, and aimed it at the back of Hennessy's head.

"In nomine Patris, et Filii, et Spiritus Sancti. AMEN."

Father Vincent pulled his knee up to his chest and, with a hard thrust, kicked Hennessy in the back. It was a smashing of violence that snapped my head up and sent me backwards to the floor.

"NEVER TRUST A HENNESSY."

"Father—"

"I WILL NOT LET YOU KILL US ALL."

Hennessy rolled over to his back to see Father Vincent marching toward him, his own gun pointed right down on him.

I frantically got back to my knees. "Father, what are you doing?"

"I'm saving your life, that's what I'm doing."

I got to my feet and ran to him. "Father, put the —"

"You SHUT YOUR MOUTH, you foolish woman. Do you not see this man bears the name? The name Hennessy? You do not belong in here. Now GET BACK." He pushed me out of the way and turned to Hennessy. "*You.* You, devil. Satan has conquered your mind."

"Take that gun off me."

"You will not make demands of your God. I tell you, oh demon, leave this body."

Father Vincent took the rosary from around his neck and wrapped it around his hand that was holding the gun. I jumped forward, but this time I put myself between the two men.

"Stop it. This is madness."

Father Vincent snatched my arm. "Do not come between the Lord your God and his fury." With all his rage, he threw me out of the way, across the room and to the floor. Then he was right back on Hennessy. "Jonah may be gone, but a Hennessy still remains. Fitting that it should be here. In this parlor, with you on the floor like this."

"You son of a bitch."

Father Vincent knelt down on Hennessy's chest and pressed the gun to his temple, smashing his head to the floor. "That's right, Hennessy. I was here. And I didn't just watch them beat your father.

I helped them. I couldn't just stand by and do nothing. No. When we had him on the ground, I did linger over your father, like I'm over you now. And I encouraged those left with me to curse him. And to pray that he'd die. It's the least I could do for the father of the Hennessys. But a monster like you needs more than prayer." He stood back up and pulled a bottle of holy water from inside his jacket and started to pour it over Hennessy's body. "Out, I say. The power of the Christ Almighty commands you. Leave it. So that when I send this body home, it may return to our Lord's arms. Or it shall return with you to the fiery depths from which it came. Be gone."

I begged him, "Father, please."

"He is no longer a man, Charolette. You heard it yourself. His thirst for blood knows no bounds. A taker of lives. Names he does not even know. A number of which he cannot tell. Well, that ends here. It ends now." He threw the bottle to the floor and stood directly over Hennessy. "You know what the last thing that passed between your father and me was?" Father Vincent looked at him, then spat in his face. "The only good Hennessy is a dead Hennessy." He cocked the weapon.

There was only one thing left that I could possibly do, so I jumped up for the table to grab the remaining gun. I made it there, but not before Father trained his gun on me.

"Woman, do not aid the devil in his demonic deeds."

In that tiny window that the gun was off of Hennessy, he sprung up and tackled Father Vincent to the floor. They fought over the weapon as they rolled across the ground. Their struggle came to an abrupt end as I came to the floor next to them and put the other gun to Father Vincent's head.

"Forgive me, Father. But let the goddamn gun go."

Father Vincent let go and remained on the floor as Hennessy stood up next to me. I didn't know who I was looking at on the ground before me. The Father that I knew and that I thought was with me wasn't what I saw. His breath was deep and wild, like a rabid animal.

"You ignorant woman," he snarled. "He is coming for us all."

"You were gonna kill Daniel."

"I was going to pass down judgment in the name of God."

"How very Christian of you," Hennessy said.

"But you were gonna murder him."

Hennessy knelt down behind Father Vincent and bound his hands behind his back.

The priest squirmed and kicked. "You silly woman. You're blind to it all. And it's all right there in front of you. Like Eve in the garden, this will all be your fault. You must believe me. Get in your place. Listen to your shepherd. You will not be spared. For no one can escape the wrath of the Lord your—"

Hennessy put a gag over the priest's mouth, though it didn't stop Father Vincent from trying to speak through it. So Hennessy dragged him across the floor to the side of the parlor, sat him up against the wall, and tied his ankles together.

"That is the last time I'm going to confession," Hennessy said.

"He was gonna kill you. You saw that, right?" I asked Hennessy.

"Yeah."

"The priest. The goddamn priest. What is happenin'? What was I thinkin'?"

"You were going to go through that door, right?" Hennessy asked me.

"I was. Right. Right." I started to feel dizzy. My knees became weak, and I stumbled as another flash, more violent than those before, entered my mind. I grabbed my head as I swayed back and forth. "Oh, god."

"Hey, sit down."

"No. I just need to think. We're not gonna die in here. I can do this. I can figure this out."

"Of course, you can." Hennessy slowly reached his hand out to me like he thought I'd need to grab him for balance. "Are you okay?"

"I'm fine." I shook my head and opened my eyes wide. "I just need space. I need to stand up."

"You are standing."

"Let me think. We're gonna make it out of here. No one else is gonna die. It doesn't have to be like this. We don't have to be like this." Everything was spinning. I dared not close my eyes again for fear of what I'd see, which made everything blur. I didn't notice where I was standing, or how I was stumbling toward the window.

"Charolette, careful!"

I had brushed the curtains that were pulled in at the edge of the window, a movement that they could see from the outside. Hennessy dove for me as a hail of bullets ripped through the side of the parlor and what was left of the window. We collapsed on top of one another, pulling each other away from the wall and barricading ourselves again behind the table. We sat shoulder to shoulder as shards of glass and splintered wood rained down on us, burrowing into each other to shield our eyes. Hennessy put his arm over my head, and I buried my face in his chest. We held there until the onslaught of gunfire finally ceased. All that we heard now were the little cracks and pops in the wood of the pierced walls and the last bit of broken glass crumbling to the floor.

"Make it stop. Please, God, make it stop. Get it out of my head. I don't want to see it anymore. This isn't real. I want it all to stop."

I noticed then how close I had gotten to Hennessy and how my hands were now on his chest. His body was warm. But I slowly pushed myself away from him, sitting upright on my own. I dusted off my blouse, and Hennessy shook the debris out of his hair. We leaned back into the table, still keeping cover, staring out into the mangled parlor.

"We're gonna die if we stay in here," I said.

"To think, I made it in and out of the Falcon Sky only to be killed right back in the place it all began." The silence that came over us felt otherworldly. Like we were thrown into some purgatory. Just waiting for the end. Hennessy asked, "Do you remember life before all this?"

I began to reflect on all the moments that had led me here. But the past was cloudy. "I remember a feelin'. A contentment. But lately I've just felt squeezed. Like I can't breathe. My mind doesn't seem to belong to me anymore."

"You must miss him. Crowley."

I didn't answer right away. My feelings weren't something I talked about, even when Crowley was alive. I didn't have many friends then. But life was good enough. It had been a series of events, and I was going through them. Life had just been going on. And I was letting it. Now here I was, sitting with a man who just pulled me down and shielded me from gunfire. Pondering the actions of a man I did not expect. A Hennessy. The thought of trusting him was getting easier. Or maybe I just thought that no one would ever ask me anything again. Whichever it was, I told him the truth.

"Miss him? No. I don't actually. At least not in the way you might think. I was fond of him. There's truth in that. But ending up with him just kinda happened, I suppose. I didn't get much say in it all. But he was a good man. A real good man. He was kind to people. And he did well to care for me. He sure did love me a lot. I could've been a lot worse off around here. There be some men with hard hearts, that's for sure. But I was safe with him. Every mornin' I opened my eyes and he'd be there. Havin' been gently movin' about, careful not to wake me. He always had that same expression when I saw him. There he'd be, nodding to me with that crooked smile of his. The way he looked at me, I could tell he'd never let anything bad happen to me. It made me wish I did love him the way he did me. But that's not a wish that came true. That sits heavy with me."

"Then why take up his badge and iron?"

"Because I owe him that. He deserved a lot better than what the people of this town gave him. He deserved a lot better from me. I'm all there is of his family. And I see . . . when I close my eyes, I see the . . ."

"You see what?"

"Nothing . . . This badge was just left to me."

"It was, wasn't it?"

I understood now that Hennessy knew far too well what it meant to have an obligation. For him, a responsibility to his brother, to his blood, shackled to him at birth, released only in death. More and more it seemed to me that maybe we were the only two who could understand each other. But he knew nothing of the fire and beckoning that came to me. Of the flames my mind forced me to see. That he wouldn't understand. I hardly did.

"What about you? You really miss the life you had before?" I asked.

"I'm here fightin' for my family's name. To set things right. But to be honest, when this is all over, when my family's safe, I hope to erase that name. Start over. Let Hennessy die in me. There's no startin' new here."

"Yeah," I agreed. I then thought of the Nightmare. "I can't believe he's gone." Even now my heart was starting to race, though I knew he was dead. I had lain awake so many nights thinking of him and what I might one day try to do. A day that now would never come. "What's it like, killin' a man?"

"It's hard to say," he said. "But it gets easier. Because you've lost that part of you that . . . I don't know. Makes you . . ."

"Human?"

"Yeah. A part of yourself dies with 'em."

"All that killin' and Jonah never found his man."

"Maybe he did. Who'd ever admit to killin' his wife? To him? To the Nightmare? We likely got him along the way. Lost in the countless others. Jonah must've known that at the end."

"I wanted it to be me. I thought it had to be. Like you said, destiny. But I'll tell you the truth, Daniel. Knowin' that your brother's gone, I don't feel that much different." My heart still ached. There was still pain. A tight grip that squeezed inside me that I hoped would have let go once I knew he was gone.

"What are ya gonna do now that you know he's dead? Will you stay here?" Hennessy asked.

"No."

"You'd leave this town without a sheriff?"

I surprised myself by smiling amidst the mayhem around us. The humor of it was not lost on me. It helped. That grip inside let up just a bit. It was over now, and I had to settle into the idea that I would no longer have to wear that heavy star anymore, trying to envision what my life could be now that the Nightmare was gone. I began to feel a warm sun and misty breeze, thinking of tomorrow. It came to me in that moment. "I'd go west. See the Pacific. I've never seen the ocean."

"Well, if I make it out of here, you'll have to let me know if you need company."

I glanced over to Hennessy's eyes and just said, "Right."

We were enjoying the moment more than we should have allowed ourselves to. We knew we were just prolonging the inevitable. There was only one way out of this and it was through that door. Into the path of men with torches and guns, who had forsaken talk of dreams and were out to rid the world of the Nightmare. A monster that was already gone. It had to be now. Before long they'd start using any means necessary to drive us out. It was clear. We were stalling.

"I think you should leave me here. Alone," Hennessy said.

"What?"

"They'll be burning this place down before long, right? No sense in you being here when they do."

"They'll do it. Even with that crazy bastard tied up in here," I said, nodding back at the priest.

"Which is why you should leave."

"I can't just leave you in here to die by a mob."

"Well then, how about you and me get the hell outta here?" Hennessy turned his body to me and looked deep into my eyes. "You said it yourself, you're done with this town. Let's bust through those doors, ride, and not look back."

"And leave it all behind?"

"Every last bit."

"To be reborn?"

"To be free."

"We won't even make it ten feet."

"Or maybe we make it all the way to the Pacific."

I felt his eyes consume me. I was weightless. A sensation came over my body like I was lying in the midday sun and the cool of moonlight all at once. No, it wasn't a smart idea to burst through the door together. It'd be death for sure. The thrill wouldn't be just staying alive or rescuing him from this situation. It was getting a chance to leave this town with someone who understood me. But that day would not be today. Though the Nightmare's life had ended, it was not yet over. And I would see it through.

"No, Hennessy. We won't."

"No . . . . Guess not."

It was time now. I had to go. We both knew it. I stood up and shook off the remaining pieces of glass. The night breeze came through the broken window and chilled me. I looked back down to Hennessy. The cold wind had reminded me how warm I felt next to him. I shook my body and dusted myself off again, though there was no glass left on me. I picked the bear claw necklace up from the rubble on the floor, held it up to him, squeezed it, and began to back toward the door. "I gotta go try and talk to them. It's all we got."

Before I could get too far, Hennessy stopped me with, "Hey . . ."

"Yeah?"

"You shot at me, didn't ya?"

"I did."

"Twice?"

After a moment I repeated, "I did."

"I thought I heard right."

"I'll see you soon."

As I reached the door I stopped. All I had to do was walk through. I raised my hand and placed it on the broken wood to push it open, but stopped right before I could. Something was keeping me from pushing through, and it wasn't the thought of what was waiting for me behind it. I took a deep breath and whipped around and began walking back toward Hennessy.

"Thank you for what you've done, Daniel. What you had to sacrifice, I know it wasn't easy. I wish things didn't turn out the way they did. I wish I got to know you better back then. Who knows how life would've turned out. I understand you wantin' ta make things right. For seein' the hold that this has on everyone. Most men would hide. But you walked right into the fray." *What was I doing?* I was rambling, trying to find the right words. I should've been walking out there, but I felt he deserved a bit of honesty. "And . . . I remember a lot more about that day by the creek when we were kids than I have led you to believe. Quite a bit actually. The smell, the colors, the warmth of the air. Just so you know, even though I hated the licorice, it was still sweet and all. I was glad you gave that to me. But I hated it. It was disgusting." I didn't know why I was saying any of it. It wasn't right. It wasn't the time or the place. But I was happy to see that that made Hennessy smile. It made me smile.

"I guess what I'm trying to say is that I'm glad." I tried to clarify. "I'm glad the nightmare is over. It's over. I'll make them see that. You have my word." I couldn't believe it, but I was now standing right in front of him. It felt so good being close to him. And as I looked on him, the parlor around me began to disappear, until only he remained. I reached out and put my hand to the side of his tired face. I didn't let his eyes grab me this time. Instead, I allowed myself to reach inside them. Then the words I was searching for finally came to me. "You know . . . maybe in another time and place. I could get lost in those eyes. You all had such beautiful eyes."

Hennessy received my words with a warm gaze looking down onto me and said, "I wish you would've told me that back then."

Everything became still. The heat I felt coming from his body turned to ice. And all around me went dark as I froze, but still managed to whisper, " . . . But I did."

Hennessy's gaze remained on me, searching my blank face. He eventually nodded and forced a smile. "That's right. You did."

It was possible that I was wrong. Maybe he just forgot what I had said back then. Though the blush in his cheeks was prominent the last time I said it. You don't forget things like that. Hennessy's eyes grew darker as he seemed to read my mind. Something wasn't right.

"Well . . . goodbye, Hennessy."

"Daniel."

"Yes. Of course. Goodbye, Daniel."

I tried to leave but couldn't get my body to move. Like when the visions of a dark silhouette and fire appeared to me by night, I became paralyzed by a fear that seized me. I noticed that

Hennessy's hand was now wrapped around my arm. It was tight.

"What's wrong?" he asked.

"I'm going to go talk to them."

The ability to move came back to me. I tried to turn away, but Hennessy kept me from doing so. I tried to yank my arm out of his grip, but his hand was stone. My arm might as well have been wedged under a boulder.

"Wait."

"Let me go," I said.

"Hold on a second."

"Daniel, let me go."

"Stop. What's happenin'?"

"You're hurtin' me."

"I'm sorry, just, wait—"

"Let go!"

"Just wait."

SMACK. I slapped Hennessy in the face. The strike echoed in the room like thunder. The rumble seemed to cause a spark to ignite behind his eyes, and his grip tightened further. I desperately searched his face, looking for that warmth I had felt in him to come back and for him to stop this. But all that was once familiar in him was gone. When Hennessy spoke again, his voice was darker than it had been before.

"I wouldn't do that again."

Though still bound on the floor behind me, Father Vincent began breathing heavily through his gag. Then he tried to push out a scream to no avail.

I tried, "Daniel . . ."

"Shhh."

"Daniel!"

"Shhh."

I tried to swing again, but I was tangled up by his long arms that were like snakes around their prey. He spun me around and pulled my body tight into his and squeezed. I bucked and kicked, tossing us around the parlor. I tried to scream as he put his hand over my mouth. We fell over onto a table, rolled off, and collapsed on the ground. I couldn't break free. Hennessy's hold was too strong. He sat us up on the floor, leaning against the wall, and hugged me in tight. The side of his face was pressed against the side of mine. I breathed hard through my nose, trying to catch my breath.

He whispered, "Oh, Charolette. We were so close. We were right there. But I never anticipated you. What a creature you are."

I tried to scream through Hennessy's hand, which was working until he slid his hand down to my throat. My attempts to call out were made silent.

"Shhh. Shhh. Shhh."

I was desperate for air. My eyes began to turn red. Off in the distance, through the windows, the faint flicking of the torches began to blur. I stretched, clawing at his hand with what little strength I could manage. Every desperate attempt I made to break free was futile.

"I guess they can't escape it. I knew this was how it was going to have to be. I'm going to loosen my grip, and you're not gonna scream."

Hennessy relaxed his grip, and my lungs filled. I sucked hard for air. Once I could breathe again, it was just instinct to try to scream. I didn't think to do it, my body just on its own tried to cry out. But Hennessy's fingers were quick to tighten, and I barely made a sound.

"No, ma'am. I don't think so."

Hennessy's gun was now right next to him. He grabbed it and put it to my head. He watched my mouth as he loosened his grip on my throat. My eyes looked over toward the barrel pressed to my temple. I didn't make a sound. My lips quivered as the cold steel sent a frigid wave across my body.

"There you go," he said. The priest was still trying to scream through the gag. "Hush now, priest." Father Vincent, like a cub looking at a wolf, went silent and cowered against the wall.

My mind was spinning. As the oxygen returned to my blood, I tried to piece it all together. None of it seemed real. I felt propelled into another world, or maybe life had just been masked with a thin veil of what I called reality, and it was now ripped from my eyes.

"He talked about you a lot when we were kids," Hennessy said.

"Daniel?"

"He did think you were pretty."

"Daniel, why are you doing this?"

"Charolette—"

"Do you not like the plan? We can change the plan."

Hennessy put his mouth right up to my ear. I remained still. Like I was now standing in front of the wolf, not wanting to move for fear of it striking. He whispered to me as if he had a secret to tell. His voice was so low and quiet, it felt as if he were speaking to me with only his mind. "There's so much to learn in the end. So much to see. People show you what they are. The more you see these moments, you begin to recognize 'em. Like him. Look at him. It's so clear. If I had a mirror to hold up to them, to show 'em how they'd look when the end comes, they'd all run away screamin'." He placed his lips right against my ear. "I really admire you, Charolette. Don't disappoint me."

In a sudden burst, I broke free from his hold and fell flat, sprawling forward onto the floor. Just ahead of me I could see the other gun. I scrambled and reached out to grab it, but just before I could lay my hand on the weapon, I felt a grip snare my ankle, and Hennessy yanked me back.

His shadow covered my body as he stood over me and kicked me in the stomach. The pain it caused me didn't affect Hennessy at all. It clearly didn't matter to him that I was a woman. It might as well have been a man that he was looking down on. He floated above me in indifference, as one who didn't care whether I lived or died. Hennessy placed his boot on my throat. I tried to push it off, but his whole leg rooted down like a tree on top of me. Clumps of dirt were breaking off his boot and crumbling around my neck. He leaned down closer to me and, again spoke softly.

"That ain't gonna get us anywhere, Charolette. Let's be honest with ourselves."

"Daniel, please."

"God, Charolette." Hennessy let out a big exhale and shook his head. "Okay," he said. He reached down and grabbed me by the hair and dragged me across the floor away from the door. My body knocked over tables and barreled through the chairs as I slid over the broken glass that was slicing tears in my skirt. He flung me around and threw me against a wall. My body bounced off and rolled back, leaving me motionless on the floor.

Hennessy walked across the parlor and picked up the other gun. He grabbed a chair and pushed it across the floor. The sound of its legs raking across the wood screeched in my ears, waking me back to life. Hennessy set the chair down in front of me. He held the gun in his lap as he sat watching my body slowly roll over. Little spots of blood were starting to appear on my body where the glass had nicked. My arms. My hands. My face. I pushed myself up and saw him sitting in front of me. I slid back against the wall.

It was perfectly clear to me where I was now. I knew the instant I reached into his eyes and watched them change. I didn't want to believe it. *It can't be*, I thought. The figure before me was darkening by the second. I feared letting him see that I knew. But it was too late. He knew all too well, and there was no hiding it anymore. This would be it for me. The thing that kept me awake at night. The moment that my dead husband had hurled me towards. The thing I told myself never to fear was finally before me. He had come at last. I was in the nightmare now.

"You're Jonah."

"I was once a Hennessy, yes."

"You've come."

"I have."

"You're the Nightmare."

For a moment, he just watched me grapple with where I now found myself and with how it was possible that I had been with the Nightmare this whole time. "What's the matter, Charolette? Am I not the monster you thought you'd see?"

"I don't know what I thought. Where's Daniel?"

"He was right about all this."

"Where's your brother? Are people in danger?"

"Are people in danger? Woman, look around ya. You're in danger. Those ain't warnin' shots comin' through that glass. That's blood on your face."

"But what about the people outside?"

"We all have our time." Hennessy looked down at the gun, admiring it. No doubt the memory of Crowley came to him as he remembered every bit of that day. How Crowley stood in defiance of

Hennessy's quest, the click of the trigger, and the bullet that ripped right through him. He was the first casualty of the Nightmare. One that would not be forgotten.

I watched him get lost in a trance. His fingers caressed the barrel of the weapon. I wondered if he planned on using that gun to kill me.

"His iron," he said. "You have your husband's iron. And his badge."

"Does it look familiar?"

"It's unfortunate what happened to Crowley —"

"Get his name out of your mouth," I demanded

"—it is. I can't say I wouldn't do it again. We're all just ridin'. Findin' our way. And all endin' up in the same place. I wish you could forget about Crowley—"

"Stop saying his name."

"—but I know you can't. It's why you're here, right?"

"I . . . don't . . ."

"It's okay. I'm glad you are. I feel like I'm finally with someone who understands me."

Holding back tears, I said, "My husband was a good man."

Hennessy sat with that for a moment, looking around the room, in what seemed to be perfect contentment. "My wife wasn't from around here, new to these parts. She was a bitch, actually. That's what my brothers said. I tried to give her flowers once, and she laughed at me. I bought her a pretty dress, and she decided to wear it out ridin'. Came back covered in dust and mud. You could never really get a hold of her. You couldn't break her. I would always ask her if she needed my help, but she never took it. It's what I loved about her. Not knowing where I stood. I wondered sometimes if she wasn't as hard as she let on. We were leavin' that day. Did you know that? We were gonna see the world. Muddy dress and all. Daniel made a toast right across the road. Steps aways from us. We shot back some whiskey and said our goodbyes. And a few moments later she had a bullet in her chest. I had never seen her eyes go wide like that. Never seen tears run down her face. She never asked me for anythin'. Until that moment. Beggin' me not to let her die. I kissed her lips. I could taste the whiskey on 'em. I told her then I would take care of her. That she was gonna be alright. She was clingin' to me hard. Tryin' ta pull herself up on me. In just those few seconds I had with her then, I realized that I never knew my wife. That girl in the wind wasn't her, just who she thought I wanted to see. I finally saw who she was. And she became more beautiful than she ever was before. Then she was gone. The last thing I did for her was lie to her. And the one time she asked for help, I couldn't. That means a minute to me. Yeah, your husband was a good man. They're all good men, Charolette. But they're not my wife."

I saw the thing that drove him. I recognized it, and I knew that he wasn't going to let anyone stop him. Certainly not me. But I did not want to die in here. And not by that gun.

"You don't have to do this," I pleaded.

"We don't sleep much, do we?"

"Please."

"We barely eat."

"Please, don't hurt anyone."

"Come on, Charolette. This is likely your last conversation, so you might as well participate. Ya see, I understand you. How does he come to ya, Charolette? He does, doesn't he? What do ya see?"

I thought of my vision of fire. And the flames traveling across the sky. The only hope I had of making it out alive seemed to be playing his game. I looked to the blood building on my hands and wiped it on my sleeve. I licked some of the blood from my lip and spat it to the floor at his feet.

"I see him. As he was when he was younger. Long before any of this."

Hennessy stared at me for a moment. As if he could see what I could see. "No," he said. "You don't."

"It's how he is to me."

"No, he isn't. I see it too, Charolette. I recognize the look in your eyes when the flashes come."

"It's what I see."

"Right. What's he saying to ya?"

It was difficult to look at him, so I closed my eyes. I squinted hard as the images came. "Ahhhh," I winced. "What is all this?"

"This? It's me trying to give y'all what y'all want. I know it's crazy, but I thought I had it there."

"Why are you doing this?"

"I thought that if I could make them believe I was Daniel and tell them the Nightmare was dead, they'd be done with it. At least I hoped they would. I see now what the priest was talkin' about. The only good Hennessy is a dead Hennessy." Turning to Father Vincent, he added, "Right, priest?"

"Why didn't Daniel just come himself?"

"That wasn't a part of his plan."

"Daniel sent you?"

"He did."

I couldn't make sense of it. Maybe I *was* blind to it all. Maybe I was naive to begin believing the Hennessys were different. I tried to summon the courage to curse them, though I feared Hennessy's retaliation. "You Hennessy boys are going to hell. I'll see to it."

"Will you now?"

"You. Daniel. All y'all involved. You'll get what's comin'."

"You might be right about that. Daniel's dead."

"Oh, I bet he is."

"He's gone, Charolette."

"You're a goddamn liar."

"He's dead. I killed him. As sure as I'll be killin' you."

Everything that Hennessy had told me before was swirling in my head, and I grappled with whether or not Daniel's journey all happened as he said it did. Riding with Jonah, the men they chased, his journey home, the story of his father. All the way up until he entered the Falcon Sky. Seeing the Nightmare before me now, I didn't know what to believe.

"If that's true, you've gone beyond what you can come back from."

"Funny, you didn't respond that way when it was Daniel killin' me. But you ain't wrong, Charolette. Far from it. I ain't tell you no lie. Daniel did come lookin' for me, that there's the truth. It just didn't turn out how he planned. He ain't a killer like you."

"That ain't me."

"It is. You just don't know it yet. I believe this is what Daniel wanted all along. It's why he really came back to find me. Oh, you wouldn't believe the things that can happen out there in the Land of the Falcon Sky."

Hennessy pointed his gun at me. My eyes went wide as the barrel aimed right between them. I fell back against the wall and held my breath as he pulled the trigger. CLICK. I was still here. No gunshot. No hole in my head. In his other hand, Hennessy held up a single bullet to me. I finally let go of my breath and exhaled. I was still alive. I tried to stop shaking as Hennessy continued to talk like what he just did was nothing.

He slid the bullet back into his gun. "Daniel just didn't want to live with it all anymore. With what all y'all've done. I could see it. Taking his life left me with a debt now. I owe it to Daniel to set this all right. No one needed to die. All y'all needed to do was listen. But we messed that up something good, you and I. I see now what Daniel wanted for this town. Why he made me do what I did to 'im. He wanted blood."

"What did you do to Daniel?"

"None of that matters now, Charolette."

His reluctance in telling me what he did to Daniel worried me. Because Daniel wasn't a monster like him. And whatever Hennessy did to his brother made me wonder, what would he do to me? This man sitting before me was nothing like Daniel as I remembered him. I knew I had to get out of there, but knew I couldn't overpower him. He sat there with his stoic demeanor. Hennessy was hiding behind something. I could see it on him. I knew it was there. There was something he wasn't telling me. I took a short breath and lowered my eyes to him.

"I'm sorry you had to do . . . whatever it was that you . . . did."

"It's what had to be done."

"Destiny," I said.

"Like destiny."

I nodded my head in agreement. Rolling over onto my knees, I slowly pulled myself up the wall to my feet. Standing in my tattered skirt, I lowered my head and softened my voice. "I think what's happened to you is horrible. You've been through a lot. Ya deserve better. We all do."

"We're beyond that."

"Maybe not. Your whole family has been done wrong. I see that. It's heartbreakin'."

"Charolette."

"I can fix this."

"Charolette."

"If ya just let me—"

"Charolette. Ya ain't leavin'."

I thought for a second, "Okay. What do ya want me to do?"

"I want—"

I bolted for the door. I could see it ahead of me and thought I could make it this time. It was right there. But as I was about to pass him, Hennessy snatched me up and threw me back to the ground. He walked over and placed his boot on my ankle.

He lifted it in the air and smashed it down. CRACK. A sharp pain shot up my leg and through my back. I moaned inside my sealed mouth, trying to mask the pain. I started moving again, now dragging myself towards the door. He watched me continue my feeble attempt to escape. With the help of a chair, I pulled myself up to standing and leaned against a table. I tried to put pressure on my broken ankle but winced as if a knife was sinking into it.

Hennessy came from behind me. I lunged like I thought I could somehow get away, but it was useless. He grabbed me and held me still against the table. From over my shoulder he said, "You'd think you'd learn to stop runnin'."

Hennessy's hands moved across my shoulders and down my back. My whole body tightened, and with each touch I felt my skin trying to push his hands away. He went to move some of the hair from my face but I jerked my head away. Hennessy grabbed me by the waist and spun me around. We were now face to face.

"Daniel was right, you are somethin' pretty."

"Get off of me."

"You know, for a second there, I thought it was gonna be you and me ridin' out of here. Not gonna lie, I liked the idea."

"That makes one of us."

"Charolette, why do you care about them? They obviously don't care what happens to you. I doubt they'd care if you screamed." I said nothing. I just stood and stared. "What? You don't believe me? Come on. Scream for me, Charolette. I saw the way you were lookin' at him. At Daniel. At me. Can you still see us? Out West? You still want to get lost in these eyes?"

I spat in his face. He laughed, then wiped it from his eyes. "You're rubbing off on her, priest. That's some guidance you got there." Hennessy watched the way hot air was pumping in and out my nose and the slight sight of my teeth perched just beyond the crack of my opened lips. "You're thinkin' about all those stories you've heard, aren't ya? About the women? Wonderin' if I was lyin'. What ta believe?" He gently ran his hand down the side of my arm. "It's been a long time, I'll tell you that. I wouldn't mind if it was you."

"Yeah?" I asked without a flinch. "And if you had me, would you be seein' your dead wife? Or would that come later?"

Hennessy turned his face away from me. His breathing stopped. Just as I began to lean away, he whipped back around, squeezing my shoulders and pulling me in close. His smile was gone. "Don't be forgettin' who I am."

"You're not real."

"I am, Charolette. Everything you've heard is true. You've failed your husband. Just like everyone else." He threw me to the ground back towards the wall.

I struggled to push myself off the floor and didn't know how much more of this I could take, of my bones slamming into the ground and wading in broken glass. I tried to pull myself back up to my feet but collapsed back into the wall. My eyes began to glaze over as the unrelenting truth was sinking in. What the falcon was bound to bring. "This can't be happening," I said.

"We're so alike, you and me."

"I'm nothing like you."

"Tell me what you see, Charolette."

"I told you what I see."

"But you didn't tell me true."

I tried to keep it together as I told him, "My mind is not your mind."

"Then why lie?"

"I'm not lying."

Hennessy lifted the gun and pointed it at me. As he did, I saw the flash of fire that screamed out in my vision. It felt as if heat was coming from behind my eyes, so I squeezed them shut.

"Open your eyes, Charolette. What do you see?"

There was another flash, and the image of the horizon came to me again. I tried to resist it. I tried to keep my eyes closed, but it didn't matter anymore. The fire was all that I could see. Even when I opened my eyes.

He asked again, "What do you see?"

"I see fire. I see the Land of the Falcon Sky. And a horizon in flames. I see the northern valley and its two high ridges darting up into the heavens. A hot blaze where all those you've killed now live. They cry out to me. And Crowley walks among them through the valley. And above him, I see the falcon. With wings made of ember. Scorching the night sky. Screeching above it all. As if it were the fire itself. Fire. I see fire and death."

"And what words does Crowley whisper?"

I closed my eyes as my husband's voice came to me. I heard it, and somehow knew it'd be the last time I ever would. As his declaration faded from me, my eyes opened, dark and sharp, piercing the shadow sitting in front of me. And I spoke the words that had ruled me since the day my husband died. The constant command speaking in my mind. "I will have vengeance," I said.

Hennessy smiled. He looked down to the gun and muttered, "Indeed, you are callin', Crowley. Indeed you are." He closed his eyes, nodded his head, and then after a deep inhale, looked back to me. "The falcon calls you. He calls the both of us."

"We're not the same."

"No? You think I'm the monster? And if I gave you this gun right now, what would you be?"

"Something else."

"Sure you would. Just like those men out there are. There are men firin' into a buildin' not even knowin' who's in it. Firin' at you, Charolette."

"I can only speak for myself."

"Let's not forget, Charolette, it was you who threw yourself in here. It was you firin' blindly. Remember? It didn't matter to you if I was Daniel or any other Hennessy. Just the thought that it could be me, that was enough. I'd say you're just like the rest of them. But they don't hear the falcon."

"I ain't killed anyone."

"Yet. And when you do, what does that make you? You look in the mirror lately, Charolette?" He bent down to me and lifted my face to his. "Tell me . . . . Is this what you see?" He held me by the chin and wouldn't let me turn away. "You know what? Let's do it. Right now. Let's end this all. Take this gun. Pull the trigger. Come on."

Hennessy grabbed the gun and came to his knees, right in front of me. He took my hand and put the gun in it. He made me squeeze the handle tight and forced me to press the barrel against his head.

He said, "Come on. Do it, Charolette. Avenge your husband. Come on! Put me to sleep. Do it!" He pushed the iron harder into his forehead. He reached out with his other arm and grabbed my shoulder, begging, "Please. Please, Charolette. Let me sleep." I could feel the barrel pressed against his skull as I watched him close his eyes. "Please," he said one last time.

From across the room, Father Vincent leaned forward to me and yelled through the gag, "Do it. Do it."

I couldn't tell whether Hennessy truly wanted me to pull the trigger. After all of the times that he might have died, should have died, did he really want it to be now? Or would this time too be added to the many tales of the Nightmare escaping death? This wild look he now had in his eyes is how I imagined the Nightmare as he lost himself riding in and out of the Falcon Sky. Death should've taken him there. Just like that night with the grizzly. There were many times he could have died, but death, it seemed, always failed to find him.

I could've ended it right then. All I had to do was pull the trigger. The gun began to shake in my hand. I waited for my husband's voice to come to me again. But nothing came.

His eyes opened on me. And as I looked to the Nightmare, his face began to shift, becoming like a mirror before me. I was looking into my own face in front of me. Then I saw myself standing in the Land of the Falcon Sky. My blouse soaked with blood. I thought that I was seeing my death. I watched myself grab my blouse and rip it off my body, looking for signs of a bullet wound. But all I saw were four great gashes across my chest, and around my neck hung the claws of the grizzly. I shook off the image and pressed the gun hard to his head but he was unmoved. I screamed, as if my calling out might summon the command for vengeance. But now, in the moment that I had been living for, the words didn't come. I closed my eyes, let go of the gun, and dropped my hands to the floor.

Hennessy lowered his arms and bowed his head, as if he thought I needed to deliver vengeance, even if it meant his death. This vengeance that had been driving us both. A word that was no longer coming to me.

He kept the iron and walked away, sitting back in the chair. "You can't be afraid, Charolette," he said.

"I'm not afraid of you."

"You gotta do like Crowley wanted ya to. It's easier than you think." Hennessy got up and went to Father Vincent. Grabbing him by the bind around his ankles, Hennessy dragged him across the room, and the priest's body slid to a halt right in front of me. "This man. He is an example of them all. Tell me he deserves to live."

Through the gag, Father Vincent said, "I deserve to live."

"Oh, no, priest. Your fate has been decided. I'm just askin' Charolette her opinion."

"Yes," I said.

"After what he tried to do?"

"He didn't know what he was doing."

"And if he had succeeded?"

"Crowley was wrong. I'm wrong."

"You're not, Charolette."

"This man doesn't deserve to die. Look at him. He's terrified. They're all so goddamn terrified. Their lives are being ruined because of the stories of one man. Because of what they believe you to be. And where has it got 'em? Look where we all are. This is insane. This is gonna kill us both. In here or out there. We're killin' each other." Careful of my ankle, I slowly brought myself to my feet and stood as strong as I was able. "We were wrong, Hennessy. I know the pain you feel. You dying, I thought would end that feelin'. But I felt no different when I thought you were dead. You made me believe you were gone, but it did nothing to me. The pain remained. You say you know me. Well, I know you. You say you see the flames and the fire in the Falcon Sky. I believe that. And that means that if I see Crowley burnin' out there when I close my eyes, then you must see her when you close yours. It's why we don't sleep. Their cries are so clear, aren't they? We can feel the heat like we're out there. But we're not. You say you've seen the falcon. But it ain't real, Hennessy. They may be tryin' to tell us something, but it ain't this. This ain't what she's tellin' ya."

Hennessy looked at Father Vincent cowering at his feet. "You think so?"

"I do."

"I do think only the two of us should be here."

"Yes. I agree. You should let him go."

Hennessy knelt down next to Father Vincent. "Would you like that, priest?" Father Vincent tried to speak, but I couldn't make out his words. Hennessy reached out and removed the gag. "Say again, I couldn't hear ya there."

The fear of having the Nightmare's eyes on him caused the priest to stutter over his words. "In the n-n-name of G-God, let me go."

"Okay. But it's dangerous goin' through that door. You might not make it."

"He'll make it," I said.

"We should have him confess first."

"Just let him go."

"I think I should offer him the same opportunity he gave me." Hennessy unbound the priest's ankles and then his hands from behind him and lifted him up to his knees. "Put your hands together."

"I'm sorry."

"No, let's do it proper now."

Father Vincent took a cautious breath, straightening his back, and tried again, "Forgive me, oh Lord, for I have sinned."

"Tell me."

"I have not been a good shepherd. I have lost my sheep to the wolves."

"You lost them? Or did you cast them out?"

"I did not help the ones that needed me."

"You failed them."

"I failed them. Forgive me, oh Lord. Please, forgive me. I was so afraid."

"How can I let you through the gates of Heaven?"

"I will repent. I will not live in fear. I will make wrongs right again. I will be a good shepherd. If you just please let me go."

"Look me in the eyes and ask me."

He could barely do it. Each glimpse he caught of Hennessy's gaze made him flinch. "Will you please let me go?"

Hennessy snatched Father Vincent by the collar and pulled him in tight. I watched his jaw tighten and teeth clench, and I thought he might pummel Father Vinent right there. But after a breath, he let it all go and said, "Alright. I guess that means you're forgiven. How easy. Let's go." Hennessy stood Father Vincent up. As Hennessy got him to his feet, he noticed the priest's rosary lying amidst bits of broken glass and rubble. He picked it up and placed it back around the priest's neck. "You might be needin' this." He patted Father Vincent's chest and then walked him to the door. "I am sad I won't be killin' you."

Father Vincent's entire body shook as he stood next to Hennessy. "Thank you. It seems my life is of the Lord's design. And no man can change our fate. Let us all remember that."

"Leave, Father," I insisted.

"The Lord intended for me to walk through that door."

"Get out of here."

"Goodbye, Charolette. I will be praying for—"

"Just go."

Hennessy began to guide Father Vincent out toward the door. "One more thing, priest. Would you be sure to see that Daniel's grave is blessed, under the Falcon Sky?"

"There is a grave? Well, of course, Hennessy. You have my word. I will be sure to journey there myself."

"Your word? Thank you," said Hennessy.

Father Vincent reached for the door. I was relieved that at least he would make it out alive. But just then, Hennessy grabbed his shoulder before he could push the door open.

"Where are you going, priest? The Falcon Sky is this way." Hennessy threw him back into the room.

"I don't know what you mean, Hennessy."

Hennessy gestured over Father Vincent's shoulder to the splintered wall and shattered window of the parlor. "Why, it's through that window."

"What are you doing?" I asked.

"I'm showin' ya, Charolette." Hennessy walked over and picked up his belt from the table and fastened it around his waist, then walked to Father Vincent and placed the other gun in his hand. "I'm showin' ya how easy it would be for the both of us." He looked at Father Vincent quivering in front of him. "Your call, priest. I want you to leave. You can either go through me and through that door. Or out that window."

"I'm just a priest, Hennessy. You know I'm not good with these tools of the devil."

"Didn't look like you were all that unfamiliar when you were pointin' it at me before. But I hear ya, priest. Let me make it easier for you." Hennessy holstered his weapon and let his hands hang empty.

Father Vincent could see his opportunity. All he had to do was lift the gun and squeeze.

"You see, Charolette. Both he and I know what we have to do. And one of us is gonna do it. The priest here ain't missin' his chance."

Father Vincent started to lift the gun slowly.

"Even now as the gun rises, he thinks he has it. He thinks he'll make it outta here alive."

"Hennessy don't," I begged.

"But he's got it all wrong," said Hennessy. Father Vincent had the gun halfway up. There was just a little more to go. "It's me who came for him."

Right then, Father Vincent quickly tried to point the gun at Hennessy. But he wasn't fast enough. Like lightning followed by thunder, Hennessy drew his gun, GUNSHOT, and a bullet pierced Father Vincent in the leg.

"No!" I screamed.

Father Vincent stumbled back, moaning in pain.

"Make the sign of the cross for me, priest."

Holding his leg, Father Vincent begged, "Please, Hennessy. Please."

GUNSHOT. Hennessy drove another bullet into his shoulder and he stumbled back again. "The sign of the cross, priest. You know you want to."

Through tears and pain Father Vincent made the sign of the cross and uttered, "In nomine Patris, et Filii, et Spiritus Sancti."

Hennessy nodded to him. "Amen." GUNSHOT. Hennessy's final bullet sent Father Vincent falling back with his body now in front of the window. An explosion of rifles went off outside the parlor, and Father Vincent was riddled with bullets. His lifeless body fell to the floor.

"You see, Charolette. Easy."

I collapsed back down on the floor and watched the blood drain from his body. Hennessy walked back over to me, still with that lingering indifference. "Why didn't you pull the trigger?"

"You weren't tryin' to kill me."

"That just makes you a coward."

"No. It just makes me not you."

Behind him, a bottle on fire came hurtling at the building and smashed on the wall near the window. The liquid spread down the side of the outside wall and flames quickly followed. Hennessy and I sat, our eyes locked on one another, as the flames began to grow around the window. Smoke was filling the room. But still, we did not move, basking in the ruin of the parlor. Just two people staring down the end of the story.

"The name Hennessy," I said. "What a curse."

"Indeed. And you. The falcon is callin'. It's time to make peace with it all. And with what you've failed to do."

The hot light and fiery glow reflected in our eyes. My recognition of my impending death overwhelmed me, and all I could do was give in to the thought that this would be my end. And with that acceptance, a conviction about the Nightmare became clear to me. I then remembered what he told me when I still believed he was Daniel. About the man who killed his wife. The one he said was lost in the countless other men. And how he hoped to know in the end that he was dead. There indeed was truth to it. As I looked on Hennessy now, I didn't just see a man who couldn't be killed, but also one who felt both pain and guilt, his image slightly skewed from the one that had haunted me. *Of course*, I thought.

My eyes sharpened on him, "What did it feel like? Killin' 'im?"

"Killin' who?"

"You know who. The man you'd been searchin' for. You said you knew it, in the end. How you got him along the way. Well, this is the end, isn't it?

"For you, Charolette."

"It's been done. Hasn't it? For a long time now." Hennessy made no reply. His silence said it all. "It didn't bring you what you thought it would. He's dead. But you just kept on. You got 'im. You son of a bitch."

"Don't worry. It'll be quick.

"Shit. This is *all* your fault."

Hennessy's eyes snapped sharp onto me. That got his attention. "What?"

"Your wife's death. It's because of you she's dead. You coulda let those men steal whatever they wanted and watched them leave. But you didn't. If you hadn't been there, she'd be alive."

"Watch yourself, Charolette."

"All of them. You kept goin' because you thought it'd bring you somethin'. But it didn't. Your brother, too. Whatever you did to him, you didn't have to. He didn't make ya do anything. You chose to. God damn, can't ya see it?"

"This won't end well for you."

"You're responsible for them both. If not for you, they'd both be here. Alive."

"I see, you want this to be painful?"

"I'm just ridin'. Findin' my way. Finally seein' where I'm headed. Listen to your wife, Hennessy."

All the light in Hennessy's eyes disappeared. It felt as if a final darkness came over the room. This was the end of my nightmare. Hennessy, rising to his feet, said, "This has gone on for far too long."

Hennessy grabbed my belt and came to me on the floor. "I'm gonna put this iron on you, I'm gonna stand you up, and I'm gonna walk across this room. Then I'm gonna put a bullet through your heart. I'm gonna do that for you, Charolette. So, when they find your body, it'll look like you tried. Like you're not just a crippled, battered woman lying on the floor in a pool of her own blood. That's my gift to you. So here's your chance, Charolette." His eyes drifted down to the star over my heart. He took joy in looking at it now. "I mean, Sheriff. I'm sorry, Sheriff. Let me help you out, Sheriff."

Hennessy lifted me to my feet. I put pressure on my ankle and screamed. The surge of pain caused me to cling to the wall. He threw the belt around my waist like he was throwing a saddle over his horse, and buckled it tight to my shaking body. He dusted me off and straightened my blouse. He reached out and adjusted the badge. "Make sure this is on good. There you go, Sheriff." Hennessy grabbed his belt and fixed it neatly as well. "And now, the final piece. Your husband's iron." He took the gun from Father Vincent's dead hand and slid it into the holster at my side. "Now you're ready to do some killin'."

I was holding back my tears, but in a sudden burst they all came rushing out. "No, no, no, Sheriff. No tears. Have some dignity," Hennessy said. He wiped the tears from my face. "Now remember, it's heavier than it looks." Hennessy stepped back, getting one last look at me. Then he yelled, "Stand up straight, Sheriff. Make Crowley proud now!"

I tried to erect myself on my one good foot and rolled my shoulders back, stopping the tears for a moment. "There you are. Now wait, Sheriff, we need to make this fair. Give me a chance to set my distance."

The fire had now grown across the wall. I watched as he left his gun at his side, put his hands behind himself, and stepped backwards, cutting through the smoke. Though the space between us was getting wider, to me the Nightmare seemed to grow larger before me. The flames cast him in a dark silhouette. I was now living in the reality that had been prophesied to me by the visions. And like in those waking dreams, I was turning again to stone, and I fought with all my might not to give in to it.

"This is it, Sheriff. Get your husband's iron ready. Don't you worry. I'm gonna help you out. I'm gonna count for ya. I'm gonna give ya ta the count of—"

GUNSHOT. Hennessy's body whipped around and flew to the floor as a bullet struck his shoulder. The ringing gunshot lingered in the room. I stood as I was before, save for the smoking barrel at my hip. The same, but not the same.

"It ain't my husband's iron," I said.

Hennessy squirmed for a moment. He reached up into his jacket and felt his shoulder where the bullet had ripped through a part of his flesh. A deep graze. My sharp aim intended only to wound him. When he pulled his hand out it was covered in blood.

He laughed. "Damn, Charolette. That was quick. Did not see that comin'." Hennessy struggled back to his feet. He moved with caution. He made no sudden movements as I had my gun trained on him the whole time. "I see we now find ourselves in a rather peculiar position. I think you just need to—"

GUNSHOT. Hennessy's hand had been drifting to his side. This bullet caused him to stumble back, and he brought his hand to his face. More blood. My aim again was true, the bullet just nicking the side of Hennessy's neck. He looked surprised by this. I stood on my broken ankle stronger than I had been before. The tears were gone from my eyes. My gun did not shake.

"You know, you really aren't at all what you let on," he said.

"No one ever is, it seems," I said.

"That badge didn't stop me before. It won't stop me now."

"The man who killed your wife. Say it. How long ago was it that you found him? Years? How long have you been ridin' in her name? And you call me the coward?"

"I am without fear."

"Ya fear admitting you were wrong. You fear redemption. Ya didn't get what ya were lookin' for out there. It pains ya. That's what's drivin' ya, not your wife."

Hennessy spat his words as he cursed me. "You know nothin', woman." Then he lowered his chin and sharpened his eyes, becoming again like the wolf, beginning to circle me.

But I wouldn't take my gun off him. I stood my ground. "I was right. You're just scared."

"I do hope your husband's watchin'. I hope he enjoys watchin' you die."

"You're not who you think you are," I said.

"Keep tellin' yourself that."

"Listen to 'em, Hennessy. They want ya to see what you have become. Your wife is callin' to ya, Jonah."

Hennessy, in a rage, grabbed one of the tables and flipped it across the room. I stumbled away as the clash sent chairs and glasses flying to the floor, but it didn't stop me from keeping the gun on him.

"Callin' who, Charolette? Jonah is gone. Crowley is gone. My wife is gone. It's only you left in the nightmare. And your blood will be the beginning of the end."

As he spoke, I watched Hennessy continue to rise taller like the flames behind him. There was no pulling him out of there. I took a breath and nodded. "So be it." I cocked back the hammer of my iron. "The next one puts you down, Hennessy."

"Does it, Charolette? Because I'm still standin'. And I can keep standin' here until this place is burned to the ground. You?"

He'd do it. It looked as if he would gladly burn now if it meant me burning with him. He studied me, his eyes turning to glassy stone, a night wolf beyond the trees.

He warned me, "All it takes is a blink. Don't blink. Don't blink, Charolette."

I extended my arm out, aiming hard. Focusing on his heart. It had to be the heart.

"Why don't I have a bullet in my head? You're gonna wait for me to go first?"

I looked down to the gun at his hip.

"It's a sick fantasy, Charolette. And you're gonna take that fantasy to your grave. Come on. Vengeance, remember? If you really cared about doin' right by your husband, you'd pull that trigger. Do it. Do it, Sheriff. Heed the falcon's call."

I swore on all the honor I had left in me. "No."

Hennessy watched as the barrel of my iron began to shake. The weight of it was getting too much to bear. I brought my other arm up and clasped the weapon with both hands.

Hennessy warned, "You know how this ends."

I steadied my breath. My palms were sweating and the gun began to slip. I felt more sure that he wanted to die, and wanted me to do it. But I was no executioner.

My aim followed him as he began to move across the parlor. "Must I remind you who I am? What stands before you? The true name I bear?"

It'd be a lie to say I was no longer afraid. I had never forgotten his name or the power that it had over me. The Nightmare. It has left scars on the walls inside my mind. They're everywhere. But that was on me. Because I had let him in. And now, it would take everything I had to finally push him out.

"You know, I've been wonderin' about that. Did you give yourself that name?"

He smiled. "Let's find out." Hennessy pulled his jacket off his shoulders and dropped it to the floor. He began to unbutton his shirt, revealing his marred chest. He pulled his shirt over his bloody shoulder and threw it to the ground. Four deep gashes had left thick scars across his heart. He dipped his hands in the priest's blood and wiped it on his face. "You wanted the monster. Well now you have it." He reached down and picked up the bear claw necklace and put it on. It seemed to sink into his body. "I told you before, Charolette. I am real. And the stories you've heard are true. People have been tryin' to kill me a long time. But I am more than just this body. I won't be dyin' today." He looked out through the window to those outside and then back to me with a smile. "Here. Let me show you."

Hennessy turned and walked towards the door. Flames were slipping through its cracks. I watched as he glided across the floor. He stopped and tilted his head up to the fire as if he wanted to feel the warmth bathe over his face. *He won't do it*, I thought. *He wouldn't make it that easy for them.* Then Hennessy in a burst kicked out the door. The fire poured into the room, blinding me.

I watched from inside the parlor as the door exploded outward when Hennessy kicked it through. His dark silhouette was framed by the flames. I could see the men outside fall back at the sight. The outdoor air was sucked inside, fueling the roar of flames as they reached out and licked the night sky, illuminating the faces, and exposing them all to the sight of the Nightmare. He emerged through the fire and into the road. Fear had turned all the men to stone, save for one who had already been running towards the building. In his hand was another bottle, burning at its top. When he caught sight of the Nightmare, with his bloodied face and shoulder, and the claws of a beast hanging from his neck, he dropped the bottle. It shattered and lit the ground on fire. The man took a few steps back and fell. The Nightmare towered over him. The man panicked to his feet and ran off screaming. There before them all, was the ghost of ash and smoke. An avalanche of terror rolled through the town.

I saw the men positioned behind wagons and hiding behind trees lift their guns and run, inside homes and out into the darkness. Like rats, they all scurried away. Hennessy moved out into the street. Not one bullet was fired. Not one man remained.

I still stood in the burning parlor. I wondered if this was going to be another one of the stories told. This time about the Nightmare massacring an entire town. When he gunned down a woman sheriff trying to avenge her husband, sending a warning to all others who dared to try the same. Whatever story it might be, none of them mattered. *I have to finish it.*

I took a step forward and stumbled. The pain in my ankle was too great. But I tried again. And again, pushing through the pain, until eventually I was dragging my ankle behind me.

My arm covered my face as I passed through the flames, a few of them singeing my cheek. Hennessy stood out in the middle of the road waiting for me. My gun was still trained on him. I left the entrance to the parlor now consumed by fire and joined him out there. I could feel the eyes of the town on me. Looking on from the shadows and the cold, dark windows. Watching. Leaving me alone and leaving me to die. But I would not look to them. *It's okay*, I thought. *We're all afraid.*

We both stood there blanketed in the night and firelight. We waited. Standing as statues in the dark. Hennessy looked at the gun pointed at him. He took a long breath and his body relaxed, like he felt a sense of peace. Scanning the windows he saw the eyes of those behind them. Like distant stars in the darkness surrounding them. He smiled. It seemed he wouldn't have it any other way.

"Look at 'em. It's exactly how Daniel said it was."

Daniel's image came to me. I wondered if this scene ever crossed his mind. A town on the verge of burning. I believed he had hoped for something better. That Jonah would've remembered who he truly was, instead of unleashing the Nightmare.

"This is why I was sent here," he called out with his breath steaming in the night air. Then he drew all his focus onto me. All of his power was now aimed right at my heart. This was the end. Then, as if he knew this would be the last thing I'd ever hear, he said, "Jonah is dead. He died out there. I am Napusai Pitsih. The Nightmare. Born again in the Land of the Falcon Sky. And I have come for you, Sheriff Charolette Crowley. I have come for all of you."

And out there, in front of the town, in the shadows of those lost, and in the path of the Nightmare himself, I said, "No sir, I don't think so." I released the hammer back and lowered my iron. I holstered it at my side. The final moment was here. No excuses now. It was just my eyes left aimed. I yelled out to him, "You're just a man."

All was still. Time stopped. The roaring of the flaming parlor reverberated throughout the street. A midnight breeze swayed my skirt gently to the side and rocked the claws back and forth across his chest. But our bodies stood like two juggernauts, rooted in the earth. Our eyes like stone.

Then, in a blink, he went for his gun, there was a BLAST, and as the sound faded out, a bullet lay in Hennessy. Gun in hand, he gazed down to see blood pouring from the hole in his chest. He looked up to me, and screaming out into the night and above the fire, he charged right for me. My open hand drummed back the hammer of my gun, letting loose all the bullets I had left. And Hennessy fell to the ground.

I stood still making sure what was down stayed down. His body lay motionless, as dust from the night breeze rolled over him. As I waited, I thought about how all of his stories would pass out of memory, fading from my mind and the minds of others. I once more caught a glimpse of Daniel. I hoped that I had done for him what he and no one else could do.

I staggered down the road, over to Hennessy, still dragging my broken ankle behind. I stood over his body. Short inhales pulsed from his blood-filled mouth as his eyes stayed wide. There wasn't much time.

"Tell me, Hennessy. What really happened to Daniel? What happened out there in the Land of the Falcon Sky?"

But his body went still. He was gone. I reached to the star on my blouse and ripped it off. In my hand the badge didn't feel as heavy as it did before. In fact, it was as if I held nothing. I knelt down and threw the badge on Hennessy's chest. The images that haunted me at night would fade away, while all that lay on the ground before me was the body of a man. I could see my bullets had hit right where I wanted. Right in his heart.

My eyes were drawn to his gun still in his hand. I couldn't help but wonder if it was empty as it had been before. I picked it up and looked inside the chamber. No. It was the end of the Nightmare. I aimed the gun to the sky. GUNSHOT.

BANGARANG!! You made it to the end!!!

I hope you enjoyed my story.

What did you think?

Leave me a review on Amazon, Audible, or Goodreads.
Hell, anywhere!

And if you really want people to know about it, tell
your friends on social media. Tell the world.

You and me, kid. Together, we'll be unstoppable!!!

Who The Hell Am I?

My name is Benjamin. I'm an actor and writer born in Southeastern Louisiana. I've spent the past two decades performing blah, blah, blah . . . . I live in NYC.

I'm sure a list of my accomplishments is interesting to some. But there are other ways to discover that.

If you made it this far, how about we say that I owe you a bit of honesty and a few things that I don't often say?

I'll tell you that I'm scared out here. These days are hard.

But I take comfort knowing that I come from a hardy stock of closeted artists and storytellers. Not by trade, but by birth. It's in my blood. And someone very dear to me refused to ever let me forget that. So, here I am.

Everyone needs story. I need story. To help discover yet again, not everything is what I thought it was. To help me change. To grow. To teach me to say the hard things. Story is the voice that tells me when to hold tight and when to let go. Story is everything to me.

Story is a woman and her iron. And when story comes to me in all these different ways . . . . I breathe and say, "Yeah. I'm gonna be alright."

For more information visit BenjaminBoucvalt.com
or follow my artistic adventures on Instagram @boucvalt.